MYSTERIES OF ANGELS

"They Were Always There!"

By
Joey Perez

WORLDWIDE
Evangelistic Ministries

www.worldevangmin.com

Mysteries of Angels: They Were Always There!

Published by Worldwide Evangelistic Ministries, Inc.
P. O. Box 51277
Philadelphia, PA 19115
(215) 331-0715

Unless otherwise noted, all Scripture references are from the New International Version of the Bible. Copyright © 1973, 1978, 1984, 1992 International Bible Society. Used by permission of Zondervan Publishing House.

Cover Design by Israel Ferrer
Edited by Weltha Wood
Proofread by Maxine Harris & Theresa Scott

ISBN 9780980106442

Library of Congress Control Number: 2009934663

Printed in the United States of America

Forewords

By Pastor Damaris Perez

I have been married to Joey for over twenty-four years and I have never seen him waiver in his faith and trust in God. As he shared the experiences he had with angels with me personally, I felt the power and anointing of God as if angels were right there in the room with us.

I even had the honor and the privilege, as I was with my husband doing a crusade with him in Newark, New Jersey, to have witnessed one of these experiences he writes about in this book. I know this powerful book on angels will bless you tremendously as you allow the faith of the Son of God to arise within you. I was so blessed by reading it and I know that you too, will be encouraged in your walk of faith, knowing that God has truly sent His angels to watch over you. God only knows, how many times angels have been assigned to deliver you from difficult times. God said in His Word that He will never leave us nor forsake us; He will send His angels concerning us. This is God's promise to us!

Worldwide Evangelistic Ministries

By Joanne Newfield

In the past twenty-four years of serving the Lord with Pastor Joey, he has shown nothing but **Faith, Courage,** and **Strength**. **Faith** when there was no money to do Thanksgiving and Christmas dinners, but we did it anyway and fed thousands of people and gave toys to thousands of children. **Courage** to go into neighborhoods and places no one else wanted to go and preach the Gospel, and **Strength** to keep on going when everyone else grew weary.

Serving God with him in these past years I have gained a lot more experience, hope, and maturity in the Lord. Pastor Joey is an extraordinary person. That is why God can use him to do extraordinary things. It is an honor and a privilege to serve God with him and the ministry God has given him.

In reading the book on angels, I think this powerful and awesome book of Pastor Joey's experiences could bring faith to people who need it and also strengthen the lives of people who need a touch from God. As it encouraged me in my life, I pray it will do the same for you.

Worldwide Evangelistic Ministries
Southampton, Pennsylvania

By Pastor Glenn Alderfer

I have been in the ministry for 40 years and was a missionary in Brazil for five years back in the 1970s and have also been a pastor for the past 32 years. I got to know Joey Perez back in the early 1980s in Philadelphia soon after he came back from Bible college in Puerto Rico. I was then involved in overseeing a ministry that Liberty Ministries had at

3054 North 5th Street which was begun by someone who turned it over to us to take men in from prisons and the streets. Joey and I did street ministry together for a while and I had the privilege of seeing him grow in the Lord, and he eventually started his own mission and ministry.

I have read Joey's new book, "<u>Mysteries of Angels: They Were Always There</u>" and I witnessed them in his life and ministry. I know that God's anointing is upon Joey to continue to do great things for God. I had the privilege of performing the wedding ceremony of Joey and Damaris when I was a pastor in Kulpsville, PA. And since then God has blessed them with two wonderful daughters. I know that God has been protecting Joey over the years and I saw how God used him back in the 1980s when we did street ministry together.

I consider it a privilege to write this forward for Joey. I thank God that I had a part in walking with him in the early days of his calling and ministry. I know that God is going to use him to reach out to many more in our beloved country as well as in many places around the world for many more years to come. I will continue to pray for and encourage Joey and Damaris in their calling and ministry.

Living Faith Fellowship
Franconia, Pennsylvania

By Rev. Donald Landis

I believe in these last days before Christ return, God is reminding us we are not alone: that He hath given us helpers in the unseen to comfort and help us in times of trouble. Psalms 34:7 says, *"The angels of the Lord encamps around those who fear Him, and He delivers them."* Psalm 91:11 *"For He will command His angels concerning you to guard you in all your ways."* Hebrews 1:14 *"Are not all angels ministering spirits sent to serve those who will inherit salvation?"*

I have known Pastor Joey Perez over twenty-five years and have seen him stay fast to the calling God put on his life, to bring salvation and healing to a needy world, to help and mature the body of Christ before His return. This book on angels is right on God's time to help Christians in times like this to be comforted and know we are not alone in our wrestling against principalities and powers.

Praise God, Brother Joey for your willingness to bring revelation on this subject at this point in time.

Jesus is Lord Ministries
Telford, Pennsylvania

By Pastor Byron Craig

Hebrews 13:2 caution us to *"not forget to entertain strangers, for by so doing some people have entertained angels without knowing it."* This scripture reminds us that angels are a part of our everyday existence. How many times have we been surrounded by miracles facilitated by angels, but we either failed to recognize these miraculous events or simply dismissed them as coincidence or acts of kindness from strangers?

Throughout the Bible, we are presented with numerous occurrences of the presence of angels. It was the angel Gabriel who revealed to Mary that she would conceive Jesus (Luke 1:28) and to Zechariah that he would have a son named John (Luke 1:11-20). Jacob wrestled with an angel for his blessing (Genesis 32:24). The Bible also assures us that God *"will command his angels concerning you to guard you carefully; they will lift you up in their hands, so that you will not strike your foot against a stone"* (Psalms 91:11-12 NIV). The Bible further reveals, *"All angels are ministering spirits sent to serve those who will inherit salvation"* (Hebrews 1:14 NIV). <u>"In Mysteries of Angels: They Were Always There"</u>, Joey Perez shared his encounters with angels and the impact of those life-binding occurrences. But it has been in his walk with the Lord that Pastor Joey is able to provide testimonies of angelic presence that has allowed him to walk authoritatively in places many men and women of God would not even consider. His courage as an evangelist, called to go to places many fear to go comes from his faith in God's protection, as evidenced by his many powerful experiences with angels.

Pastor Joey explores his personal experiences regarding the presence, protection, and visions given by angels. He delves into the role angels have played in different points of his life, preparing him for the plans God had for him and at times, shielding him from danger before he even accepted Jesus Christ as his personal Savior.

This book will take the blinders off your mind regarding angels! If you do not believe that they exist in the modern world, you will be challenged to rethink that view. For those who believe in the existence of angels on earth, it will allow you to be more aware of miracles, small and large.

It is my hope and prayer that you receive all that God has purposed for you to get by reading this book. I pray you will be enlightened and encouraged by Pastor Joey's testimony and open to experiencing your own miraculous moments!

Macedonia Baptist Church
Norristown, Pennsylvania

By Dr. B. J. Pruitt

In reading Pastor Joey's book I believe I need to preface this forward with this statement: "I personally believe in angels." In fact, I believe that most people believe in angels in some way or another. So when I read that Joey believes that angels are dispatched for our protection, I have no problem with that. The Bible says, *"For he shall give his Angels charge over you, to keep you in all your ways"* (Psalm 91:11). I realize this prophecy was given directly concerning the Lord Jesus Christ. However, the Word of God is for all people in every generation. In the late 18th and early 19th century, there was very little interest in angels among

Christians and church leaders in America. But with the dawning of the 20th century, minds began to unbend and hearts began to open. From then until now we have witnessed a great revealing of the ministry of angels.

Stories from the Bible started to come alive. We read of Paul's encounter with an angel when they ran into a great storm. Fear gripped the men on the ship and havoc was everywhere. It was quite evident that everyone was in danger of losing his or her life. Everything that could be done had been done, "all hope that we should be saved was then taken away," Paul stood and declared, "There shall be no loss of any man's life among you, just the ship. For there stood by me this night the angel of God, whose I am, and whom I serve, saying, 'Fear not Paul; God has given you all them that sail with you.' Wherefore, sirs, be of good cheer: for I believe God, that it shall be even as it was told me." Paul was giving the angels their just recognition. Of course it was God who had dispatched them, in this way he was giving God the glory.

We must learn to give honor where honor is due. The angels, and not even Jesus Himself, will not take any honor upon himself, which belongs to God. Paul in describing the work of angels said, *"Are they not all ministering spirits, for service sent forth, on account of those who are to inherit salvation?"* (Hebrews 1:14). The allusion is generally to their office of subordinate ministration in furtherance of the Divine purposes of human salvation.

I have personally known Joey Perez for twenty years or more. I have ministered with him and for him.

His ministry speaks for itself. However, I believe I can speak for him in recognition of the work I have witnessed take place through him. When I think of Joey, I think of Joseph in prison, and Daniel in the Lion's den, and the Hebrews in the fiery furnace, and Jeremiah in the pit. All of these things I have seen him go through (not literally), but circumstantially. And he has come through each and every one of them in victory. I have seen him knocked down, but never knocked out.

In conclusion I would like for us to return to the night when Jesus was betrayed. Remember when one of His companions sought to protect Him from the soldier of the high priest. Jesus said, *"Put your sword back in its place. Do you think I cannot call on my Father, and he will put at my disposal more than twelve legions of angels?"* (Matthew 26:52-53). It is the Father in heaven who hears the cry for help, who commands His waiting angels to contact us. We can only contact angels through Him. They are His messengers, His servants, not ours unless He commands. But we can call and expect an answer. Pastor Joey is not being presumptuous but exercising his right as an heir of salvation.

Frontline Ministries
Valrico, Florida

TABLE OF CONTENTS

CHAPTER 1

The Angel with the Whistle

When I was about nine years old, growing up in North Philadelphia, I lived in a neighborhood that was predominantly German and Irish; there just weren't many Hispanic or African-American families. Every Saturday a few of my friends and I would go to Fairmount Park where the Philadelphia Museum of Art is—the one made famous in the <u>Rocky</u> movies. We would take our fishing rods down to the Schuylkill River where we tried to catch catfish.

I remember one particular day, about nine or so of my friends and I went fishing together. The group included Joey, Kevin, Louie, Barry and his brother Labell, my brother Mikey, two other guys who lived in our neighborhood—and me. We must have caught close to ten catfish, but instead of keeping them, we threw them back into the river. As we were fishing, fifteen or more other guys suddenly appeared out of nowhere, surrounding us and forcing us into a circle. They began to demand our money. These guys were ready to beat us up with their sticks, bats, and knives. They were probably from West Philadelphia, about a quarter of a mile from where we were.

They started asking us questions such as what gang we were from and where we lived. They had already taken all our money and our jewelry—and we were scared. We were in a remote place with no one around and no place for us to run. Suddenly, their leader looked straight at me and for no apparent reason said, "You get out of here!" He told me to run off before they started beating up the other guys. I started to do just that, but I stopped as I realized Mikey was still there. I told them Mikey was my brother.

"You two—run! Hurry up before we beat you down!"

Mikey and I didn't wait for him to change his mind! We started running up the hill. The guys from the gang watched us go. Then they turned back around and started beating our other friends, even though my friend Louie—a strong, cocky guy— actually tried to pick these guys up and fight back! While Mikey and I were making our escape, we saw a police officer who seemed to appear out of nowhere. As we approached him, he started to blow his whistle. We told him that a gang of guys were beating up our friends. As he looked down the hill at what was going on, he blew his whistle three times.

What Man?

When the gang that was beating up on our friends heard the whistle, they stopped what they were doing and started to run away. The cop blew the whistle another three times, and that gang began to run even faster. While they ran off, my brother and I raced down the hill to help our friends who were lying on the ground after being beaten up. After asking them if they were all right, we turned around to look for the police officer—and he was nowhere in sight! I asked the rest of my friends what had happened to the police officer who had come down the hill with us.

"What police officer?" they asked, "We never saw one!"

I explained that there was a police officer who had blown his whistle three times, and again, they told me they hadn't seen anything of the sort.

Today I find myself asking this question: was that policeman—who appeared for a second and then disappeared—really an angel sent by God? Were my brother Mikey and I just seeing things? Did we just imagine that there was a man who looked and acted like a police officer? I don't believe we imagined anything; I believe God was demonstrating His love that day by assigning an angel to protect us. We could have been seriously injured or even killed.

I thought about this experience frequently as I was growing up. I knew I had seen a police officer, but when I turned around to see if he was following me, he was gone. I didn't see him again. No one else had seen him or heard the whistle. Today I am *sure* he was an angel sent by God to protect my brother and me. In just one of the many passages in the Bible concerning angels, Hebrews 13:1-2 declares this: "Keep on loving each other as brothers. Do not forget to entertain strangers, for by so doing some people have entertained angels without knowing it."

An Angel Assigned to You!

Angels are real. As you read the Bible, you will come across many instances where angels were sent by God to minister to people; to give them divine messages; to warn, protect, and guide them; to work on their behalf—and on one occasion, to set them free from prison! God has assigned angels to us for our protection and benefit. The angels mentioned in the Bible really do exist—and I have evidence in my own life that they do!

Chapter 2

I Should Have Died Three Hundred Times

"Are not all angels ministering spirits sent to serve those who will inherit salvation?" (Hebrews 1:14)

A question I have often been asked by my daughter, by other believers, and even by unbelievers is, "Do you believe angels are *real*?"

My answer has always been a resounding, "Yes!"

I experienced so many close calls in my past when I was an unbeliever. I didn't know God. I didn't even know if there *was* a God, and I certainly didn't believe in the devil. But when the Lord gave me a new life and a new spirit—His Holy Spirit—all of this changed. My eyes were literally opened. Today I understand why I am still alive even though I should have died hundreds of times over. Instead of allowing me to die, God demonstrated His mercy toward me by sending angels, which I didn't even know existed, to deliver me from danger.

Growing up in the city of Philadelphia as a gang leader and a drug dealer, I frequently had friends who were in the gangs with me say, "Joey, someone is with you!" Somehow they realized there was some form of supernatural protection over my life. Once, I was knifed seventeen times and when I took off my coat, it was all torn up. There were holes in the front right over my heart, in the collar where the knives should have entered my neck, and about ten holes in the back. I thought I had just been punched hard, but I had been stabbed—without the knives ever entering my body.

Looking Death in the Face

On another occasion, I was chasing some members of a rival gang without realizing that I was being set up. This gang—the 8th and Diamond Gang—sent two guys around the corner to where my gang and I were hanging out. They knew that once we saw them, we would chase after them because our gangs were rivals. Sure enough, their set-up worked, and we started chasing them. I was ahead of the three guys who were with me—Larry, Barry and Becote—as we ran after them down Germantown and Diamond Streets. As I came around the corner onto Diamond going west, these two guys ran north, turning right onto Marshall Street.

I was reaching out to grab one of them when I heard Larry yelling, "Joey, grab him, *grab him!*" Just as I got close enough to the nearest gang member, another man jumped out of the alley and pulled a pump-action shotgun on me. As soon as I saw this guy come at me, I froze right in my tracks. I knew instantly that I was facing death. Many things ran through my mind at that moment—and one of them was that I was going to die *that day*. The man with the shotgun tried to shoot me, but the gun wouldn't work—the action had stuck. He kept trying to shoot, but the shotgun still wouldn't fire. Once my attacker realized there was no way he could get the shotgun to work, he ran off, leaving me alone.

Was this just luck that the shotgun jammed? And the day that I was stabbed seventeen times without a knife piercing my body—was that luck too? I used to see people walk around with a little rabbit's foot on their key chains, and I would ask them why they did that—what was it for? Everyone told me that it was for good luck. I'd tell them it was probably good luck for them but not for the rabbit because he was dead! Many times we think the good things that happen in our lives take place just because we are "lucky." I know better—I know it wasn't just "luck" that saved me but God's merciful intervention through the angels He sent to protect me.

Indian, Ancestor, Ghost?

I remember living a life of sin when I was around eighteen years old, filled with violence and crime. I had just gotten out of prison and was terribly confused by an experience I had in prison just before my release. A guard had come to my prison cell and described everything that was going to happen to me-the court was going to drop some of the charges against me, and I would be getting out that week. This guard told me these things on a Monday, and for the rest of the week, I kept looking for him, but I couldn't find him anywhere. However, by the end of that week, everything he told me would happen, *did* happen!

Was that guard some ancestor of mine or a ghost from the past? Back then I had no idea what was going on, no understanding of God's ways and how He was already working in my life. I thought that guard was a guardian Indian or a relative come back from the dead to protect me from danger. This is what I had been told as a child. Was that true? No, of course it wasn't. Now I know all those "explanations" were really lies from the devil. They were lies meant to keep me from knowing, loving, and serving God.

No Idea What to Believe

Two days after I was released from prison, I celebrated by partying at a discotheque. I was drunk, supposedly having a good time. However, I wasn't enjoying myself at all because my sin haunted me day and night. All the things I had done—violent crimes I'd carried out as a gang leader and drug dealer—were always before my eyes, just as the Bible says in the Old Testament about King David's sin of adultery and murder being right there in front of him. I couldn't get away from what I'd done. It filled my mind and followed me wherever I went.

As I was sitting in the discotheque that night, some men approached me and asked if I was the leader of the Midtown Zulu Gang. When I stood up and replied that I was, twenty men suddenly surrounded me. Once again I knew that my life was certain to end—they had guns, knives, and broken bottles. Seeing this, I heard a voice in my mind (which I now know was an evil voice) saying to me, "If you're going to die, die tough!" I knew I wasn't Superman, but I started to fight, hitting the leader right on the nose. He fell to the floor. I turned around and, with strength I didn't know I had, grabbed a young man, lifted him up in the air, and threw him on top of seven other guys who fell to the floor as well.

"Kill me, kill me!" I screamed at the top of my lungs as I kept swinging, "I'm not afraid to die!"

When their leader hauled himself up from the floor, he just looked at me, saying, "I have *never* seen a man as crazy as you! You got my respect!"

I didn't care if I had his respect or not. That night I was furious and filled with violence because of the anger and bitterness in my life. I couldn't understand why no one hit me. Even as I turned to walk away, I expected to be stabbed or shot from behind—but it didn't happen! Once more I asked myself if this was luck or the guardian Indians I had been taught about as a child. Back in those days, I didn't know *what* to believe.

Now I understand that God had a purpose for my life. When God has a purpose and a destiny for a person's life, He will do whatever it takes to protect that individual. He will do whatever is required to open that person's eyes to see that they have not made it through life on their own, that God has sent His angels on their behalf.

The Bible is very clear on the subject of angels. Psalm 91:11-12 explains: "For He will command His angels concerning you to guard you in all your way. They will lift you up in their hands so that you will not strike your foot against the stone." I believe this Scripture is for Christian believers, but I also believe that when God has a purpose for a man or a woman, He will send angels to protect and watch over them. Even though a person is separated from God because of his sin, many of the dangers he has been delivered from in his sinful life are because God has been demonstrating His mercy. Of course, the unbeliever is blind to this truth.

The Voice of the Devil

One more great deliverance took place in my life while I was still living in sin. I had been constantly tormented in my mind. Not too many people liked me and I felt the same about them. I hated them and my heart was filled with anger. Whenever I walked past people who were not involved in gangs, drugs, and violence as I was, I was convinced that they were talking about me—and not saying anything good either. Often I heard what they said about me—some of it was true, some wasn't. This began to torture my mind.

One day while I was at home doing drugs, I started being tormented by an evil spirit. This spirit came to me, telling me that everyone hated me and wanted me dead. When I would walk through the neighborhood where I hung out with my friends, I'd see a group of guys on the corner who were different from me. Seeing them laughing, I was convinced they were laughing at me. This went on for a week or two. Then when I was by myself, walking or driving home or just lying in my bed, I would hear this spirit telling me I needed to let everyone know that they were going to respect me one way or another!

The voice from that evil spirit tormented me so much one day that I took my gun to the neighborhood where I used to hang out. I intended to shoot all the guys on that corner—about seven or so. But as I got out of my car, something happened to me. It was as if something left me—and when it left, I felt such peace that I didn't understand what I had been doing. It was as if something had left my body, and I had come back to my senses. Now I understand that God sent His angels to deliver me from the tragic mistake I was about to make that day. This wasn't the first time I had experienced something like this, where I had thought about walking up to a corner and shooting everyone on it. It had happened a couple of times before that.

As a minister, I now realize that God had a plan for my life even back then. If I had committed that crime when I was eighteen, I might be in jail from then until today—and perhaps for the rest of my life. The Bible tells us plainly in Psalm 34:7, "The angel of the Lord encamps around those who fear Him and He delivers them." You might ask how this could happen to people who don't know God, who call themselves atheists, pagans, and even sinners. How can they fear someone they don't know? That was the life I lived. I didn't fear death. I jumped in front of rifles, pistols, and shotguns when we fought other gangs. I ran up in front of people who were trying to stab me, yelling at them to go ahead and kill me. I had no fear of death or God whatsoever.

But God, through His grace and immense mercy, helped me understand that even though I was a sinner who did not fear Him, He had sent His Son to die for me. Jesus had shed His blood to cleanse me of my sins and make me a new creation. He sent His angels to protect me even when I was lost in my sins. Today I *know* angels are real. I know they exist. I know that when I get on my knees to pray and call on the God of the heavens and the earth—the God of the entire universe—He answers my prayers. The Bible also says that the prayers of the children of God are always before His face as His angels take those prayers to Him.

God Has Sent His Angels for You

I have written this book to share with you the encounters I have had with angels since I came to the Lord Jesus Christ. It is my hope that as you read this book you will be edified and strengthen in your walk with the Lord Jesus Christ. You can be assured that He has given His angels charge concerning you! What a wonderful promise we have in Him!

CHAPTER 3

God's Angels - Our Protection

On June 7, 1979, I gave my life to God. Previously my state of mind was such that I had decided to kill a whole list of people and then kill myself—that's how my life was going to end. God had other plans for me—in His mercy, He gave me a second chance in life. After I became a Christian by surrendering my life to the Lordship of Jesus Christ, a fire began to burn in my spirit! I wanted to go back to the same communities where I had lived and hung out, selling drugs and engaging in gang war, trying to kill the people who were trying to kill *me*. My heart, once so hard and full of evil, was now a heart of human flesh, and I was able to understand that many others were experiencing the same pain and emptiness I had once known.

I returned to my old neighborhood with a vision that one day I would go into other cities and even other countries all over the world, preaching the Gospel of Jesus Christ. I began holding street meetings after knowing the Lord for only six months. As I held these meetings, I began to have some of the same experiences that I had had as a gang leader. People were still trying to shoot me! Others would walk across the street and pull knives on me while I was preaching on street corners because they didn't want me talking about God. Even though I was under this physical attack, I had no fear of dying. I believed that if God delivered me from danger in my past life of sin, He would deliver me even more as I lived a life where I wanted to do what was right before Him.

On August 19, 1980, I went to a Bible college on the island of Puerto Rico. That was an incredible experience for me. Even though I am of Puerto Rican ancestry, I was born and raised in the city of Philadelphia, and I didn't know how to speak Spanish. I barely understood any of the language. My pastor, however, felt in his heart that God wanted me to go to this Bible college in Puerto Rico. I trusted this man of God, the Reverend Victor Manuel Uyola, so very much. This was another miracle because I never trusted anyone in my past. I decided whatever he said God wanted me to do, I would do it. I believed in my heart that God was using this man to guide my life. That is the role of a pastor-to guide, instruct, teach, oversee, and command us by the Holy Spirit of God in the way we should live.

Stay Still

When Pastor Uyola told me that he felt in his heart God wanted me to go to Puerto Rico, I said I would be glad to do it. However, once I got to Puerto Rico, I began to experience great struggles. I didn't adapt well to the courses I was taking because I couldn't understand the teachers who taught everything in Spanish. In my room at night, I would lie in bed asking God if this was really where I belonged. I started to doubt and wondered if I had been sent here by mistake. Why would God send me to a place where I could barely understand the language? God, however, knows everything! The Bible tells us that He is omniscient—all-knowing. He knows the purpose for our lives and what He can do with us if we will yield ourselves one hundred percent to Him and allow Him to be the Lord of our lives.

I began to pray even more, believing God would hear me if I asked Him for help. Every morning for the first three weeks that I attended this Assembly of God Bible College in the Santa Monica area up in the mountains of Puerto Rico, I would wake up at four in the morning. I couldn't sleep. I didn't have any peace. As I kept tossing and turning, I decided to get up and pray—but I wouldn't pray very long because I was frustrated and discouraged, feeling I was out of the will of God. I even thought about just leaving and returning to Philadelphia. I didn't; I had learned that God would use whoever He placed before me as a guide for my life.

Somewhere around the fourth week of school, I got up to pray and felt in my heart that I should speak to the Dean of the school. He wasn't available so I went to Assistant Dean Manuel Rodriguez and began to tell him my problem.

"I'm not adapting very well. I'm confused, I can't sleep at night, I wake up at four in the morning and toss and turn for an hour. Then I get up and pray, but I can only pray for about a half an hour or maybe forty-five minutes. I don't feel God is answering my prayers. I feel like leaving—I don't feel like staying here! It's like there is a battle for my life, like there is an evil force constantly trying to move me out of here. But, at the same time, I also feel this great peace within myself that is telling me to stay still. Whenever I feel this inner peace, I hear a still, small voice telling me to stay still because God has a purpose for my life!"

"Joey!" brother Manuel said, "I believe very strongly in my heart that God is waking you up in the mornings. I also believe He brought you here, and He wants to use you powerfully in the future to reach people who are like you used to be, as well as, many people from all walks of life. He wants you to get up early and pray. The chapel is on the first floor of your dormitory. The doors are always open—we never lock them. When you get up, why don't you just go down to the chapel and pray?"

I told him I was going to do that. After being in school for about a month, I would get up at around four in the morning, wash up, get dress, and go to the chapel to pray. I began to develop a stronger prayer life. I began to feel better and my surroundings were becoming more peaceful. Every time I prayed, I would ask God to help me and give me the strength to make it through the school; to give me wisdom, revelation, knowledge, and understanding; to show me how to read, speak, and understand Spanish so I could communicate better with those around me.

The Sound of Angel Wings

Each morning I would go to the chapel, walk up to the altar, lie down and pray. This particular morning while I was praying, I had an experience that left me amazed at God. The chapel was very dark because it was early in the morning and still dark outside. As I was praying, a bright light lit up half of the room. It came from my right, and I thought someone had walked into the chapel. I thought it might be Manny who was from New York or Orlando who was from

Ohio. They were friends of mine who also spoke English and I felt comfortable around them.

When I lifted my head to look around, the light disappeared and everything became dark again. After I prayed for about an hour, I saw the light streaming through the windows, but I continued to pray. Suddenly, I heard something that sounded like wings flapping. I didn't lift my head to look but instead became quiet. I heard these wings flapping three times when suddenly, a wind came into the room. I still didn't move—I was scared to even look to see if anyone was there. I simply stayed quiet, listening to the flapping of those wings.

As I listened to the sound of the wings, a great peace came into the chapel. After a while I got up to look around, but I didn't see anyone. I kept on praying and began to feel as if someone were walking around the room. I got up again and looked around, but no one was in the room. Even though I didn't see anyone, I felt deep inside my spirit that whatever had walked into the room was of God.

"Is the Lord here? Has He sent His angels?"

I continued to pray, finishing around six thirty in the morning. By that time, the rest of the students had come in to pray, and I began to pray with them. According to the school's rules, we had to pray from six thirty to seven each morning before doing our chores and having breakfast. I had no idea that this was only the beginning of the supernatural experiences I would have with the Lord at this Bible college, where I was preparing myself for the ministry to which God was calling me.

I shared this experience with others in the school, and it encouraged many of them to come early to join me in prayer at five in the morning. After about two months; however, I was by myself again. God always woke me up because He wanted me to develop a strong prayer life. As I continued to pray, my relationship with God was growing. I began to understand His voice and became more sensitive to what He wanted me to do.

Around October of that year, I felt strongly impressed of God to hold a crusade in Royaltown, Bayamon. This community had terrible problems with drug addicts and dealers. The crime rate was high, with people frequently killing one another. Even though I barely spoke Spanish, I felt the inspiration of God to hold this crusade. I told the college Dean, Carlos Osorio, that I believed God wanted me to do a one-day youth rally in Royaltown. I wanted to invite many churches to back us up as we went into that area. Dean Osorio was from New York and spoke very good English. He shared his testimony with us, telling how he had been a heroin addict for many years when God saved him while he was shooting up drugs on the thirteenth floor of an old apartment building in the projects. When I told Dean Osorio what I was sensing in my heart, he knew it was the Lord and told me that he would back me up.

The Presence on the Altar

We began going to churches in the area, seeking their support, and on November 15, 1980, we held the youth rally. There were about eight hundred people present, and many of them from that neighborhood were bound by drugs or had a criminal background. I began to share my testimony, speaking in English while a young girl interpreted what I was saying in Spanish. As I was speaking, I sensed in my spirit that someone had just gotten up on the altar. I continued to speak, but I looked around to find if I could see anyone. Although I saw no one, I knew whoever was on the altar was good and of God because there was such peace within me.

When I gave the altar call that night, many young people came forward to be saved. Young girls who were messed up in drugs came forward crying. I was so blessed that night as I saw people coming for salvation, experiencing the presence of God. I had a strong confidence that I was surrounded by angels. Later, when I returned to the school that night, I shared with the other guys what I had felt, and they told me that there was a great peace and a "good presence" there that night. Even though there was a language barrier, people had come forward sobbing and weeping to be saved. This was the second time I had experienced the presence of God's angels around me, and it gave me confidence in Him.

I began to feel led of God to go to many other cities on the island. I started preaching in churches that wanted me to go out into the streets to the most violent communities. As I preached on the street, people came up behind me with knives trying to stab me. Instead of harming me, they would fall to the ground, dropping their knives. People would approach me, angry at what I was saying, trying to hit me. But, as they came near the altar, they would "freeze" and fall to the ground. During these meetings I began to experience the power of God in a way I had never known before. The anointing of God—His power to save and deliver—was on my life in such a strong way that as I spoke, people would be healed and set free. Every time I gave an altar call, people would come forward, weeping in repentance.

I was invited to speak in a church in the town of La Monja, Barrio Obrero in Santurce, Puerto Rico. Everyone told me it was a dangerous place, but I didn't feel any fear there. I knew God was with me and He had His angels there to protect me. When I spoke, I would feel their presence on the altar. I knew He was protecting me. If He had kept me alive during my violent past, He would certainly guard my life now. As I spoke in this church, I noticed that the doors were closed with iron bars. I had never seen anything like this and wondered why the church did this. I found out later it was because of fear that criminals would enter the church—and this was a church that believed in God and in His power!

As I gave my testimony, I saw two men standing at the door. They were making certain moves at the back, but I didn't understand what they were doing. Finishing my testimony, I gave an altar call. No one came forward. When I asked the two men at the front door if they wanted to receive Jesus as their Savior, they said, "yes." I asked one of the deacons to open the door. He removed a lock, opening these metal doors that looked like a prison gate. When he did that, the two men ran into the church. One ran to the altar where I was standing, and the other one stood at the back of the church and got up on one of the pews, yelling at the people. Naturally, the congregation became frightened!

After the service was over, people told me that these men came to the church just to treat the house of God with disrespect. When I looked at the man who had run up to the altar, I noticed he wasn't looking at me. I asked him if he wanted to receive Jesus as his Savior. He looked vicious and violent, and he still wouldn't look me in the face. Suddenly, he yelled out to me, looking at the floor, screaming, "No, I want you!" As soon as he said that, he began swinging as if he was going to punch me, just like a boxer dancing up and down in the same place. Again I asked him if he wanted to receive Jesus as his Lord and Savior. Again he yelled, "No, I want you! I want to beat you up!"

When I heard that, my natural instinct was to defend myself. However, I heard this peaceful voice in my spirit say, "Do not fear, for I have given you power over these spirits!" When I heard this, I told the congregation not to be afraid of these men. I kept watching the one at the back who was yelling. I thought he had a gun, and he was intimidating the people in the church who were all backed up against the wall, frightened of him. These men kept saying that they wanted me, that they were going to kill me— "kill the preacher."

Safe From the Enemy's Attack

Suddenly, I walked up to the one in front—who still couldn't look at me—and grabbed him by the hair. I laid my hands on him and said, "In the name of Jesus, devil, you come out!" The man fell to the floor, and then he bounced back up again and ran out the door. When the congregation saw that, they began to praise God. I walked up to the other man who was probably six feet tall and was standing on the pew. I got up on the pew myself and grabbed him by the neck with one hand and put my other hand on his head. When I laid hands on him in the name of Jesus, he also fell to the floor, jumped up and ran out of the church. The people in that church began to glorify God for the great things which had taken place. As I went home, I was both amazed and puzzled. I felt a constant presence around me as if I was never alone, as if someone was there with me. Someone was protecting me. Every day I had peace in my heart that God had angels protecting me wherever I went.

I began to have more of these experiences throughout my time in Bible college. Whenever churches invited me to preach in their communities, they would always ask me to preach on the streets. I began to preach in areas where I *knew* God had to be with me to protect me. I went into areas where even the police would not go because of the violence.

After I finished my first year of Bible college, I asked the Lord if I could live outside the school during the second year. I wanted to have more freedom to travel in the evenings after I had finished the school day and all my work. I felt such peace in my heart that God was directing me this way. I asked my uncle (my father's older brother Saul Perez) who lived not too far from the Bible college if I could live with him. He agreed, and I went to live with my uncle, his wife, and his son who were all attending a Seventh Day Adventist church. I would share with them the things that happened each time I went to a different church—and whenever I returned from a service, it was with a carload of vegetables and fruit that the church people had given me! However, as I asked God what my future ministry would be like, I felt a strong burden in my heart to help those in need and to reach the drug addicts, prostitutes, and those who were possessed by evil.

Dreams and Visions

Around April of 1982, just as I finished my second year at the Bible college, I had a dream one night. In that dream I found myself standing in front of the door of an enormous building. It looked as if it was either a two-story building or a split-level, and it must have been around 80,000 square feet. Standing in front of this building in my dream, I heard a voice, filled with peace, speaking to me from behind.

"Look and observe what I am going to show you."

Suddenly, the doors of that building opened, and the voice said, "Walk in." I moved closer to the door and the voice commanded, "Step inside." Upon entering the building, I noticed steps going up and others going down. The steps leading downward seemed to go to a basement. The steps leading upward appeared to go to offices. I walked up those steps and saw a woman sitting right in front of me at an oval table in what appeared to be a reception area. Looking to my right, I saw a number of men and women working at computers. I heard other people entering the building, and when I turned around to look behind me, I saw four men. They had several stacks of mail strapped with heavy rubber bands.

As they walked into the building, I heard the voice again.

"This is the support that will come from all over the United States and other countries." Then I looked over to my left and saw a hallway with several doors leading to what appeared to be many classrooms. The voice said to me, "Go back out."

I was really surprised walking down the steps to leave, that the doors opened outward. This was the opposite of what happened when I walked in; the doors had opened to the inside, but now they opened outward. When I was about fifty feet from the building I stopped, turned around and looked at it again. Then the voice said, "This is how your ministry will be. It will reach many people in all walks of life. You will prepare people for the ministry that I'm about to put into your hands, and all these people will be working for you."

When I looked again, I saw fire coming down from Heaven into the middle of the building. It didn't burn the building although it kept coming down. Then the doors opened again, and I saw the fire coming out of the front door of the building—and it was coming toward me. When it got to about four feet from me, it stopped and went to the right and to the left.

The fire hovered about five feet off the ground and kept moving down the street. I watched as it moved to the left and to the right. Then I heard the voice again.

"This is how your ministry will be. I am going to pour so much fire into your ministry that it will not only come into your building, but it will go out the doors from the people whom you will prepare in this building for ministry. They will come out of this building with fire! The fire will not only sweep the city you live in— Philadelphia—but it will sweep to many other cities all over the United States, and you will even go to other countries full of this fire that I will pour into your ministry."

Suddenly, I woke up—and I couldn't go back to sleep. It was around four in the morning; I got up and began to pray. But the dream bothered me. How was this going to happen? Would I be able to handle it? God; however, never fails! He always speaks forth to confirm. In Joel 2:28-30, God speaks through the prophet saying:

> **"And afterward, I will pour out my Spirit on all people. Your sons and daughters will prophesy, your old men will dream dreams, your young men will see visions. Even on my servants, both men and women, I will pour out my Spirit in those days. I will show wonders in the heavens and on the earth, blood and fire and billows of smoke."**

God speaks through dreams and visions to inspire and anoint His people to bring forth His purpose in their lives.

This was quite an experience for me! I didn't even know what a vision was since I grew up lost, with no sense of direction in my past. Now I was a Christian, and God had visited me with a supernatural dream. At the time, I had only been saved three years, but I was experiencing the spirit realm and God's power in a way I had never known existed. All of this was to prepare me for the work to which God was calling me. His angels had protected me in the past and they continued to protect me because God had a purpose for my life.

Just like in the Bible

I shared this dream with the Dean of our Bible College and with my friend, Manny. When I told them what God had shown me, they rejoiced, telling me that God was preparing me for "something powerful." Before God can entrust someone with a ministry that will bring Him glory, He will first try and test them, break and mold them so that they can do everything according to the will and purpose that God already ordained before the world began. The Dean told me of stories in the Bible where God spoke to people through dreams and visions. He told me about Daniel and Jacob and I also began to do my own reading on those stories. One that really caught my attention was how the Lord spoke to Jacob in Genesis 28:10-14:

"Jacob left Beersheba and set out for Haran. When he reached a certain place, he stopped for the night because the sun had set. Taking one of the stones there, he put it under his head and lay down to sleep. He had a dream in which he saw a stairway resting on the earth, with its top reaching to heaven, and the angels of God were ascending and descending on it. There above it stood the Lord, and he said: "I am the Lord, the God of your father Abraham and the God of Isaac. I will give you and your descendants the land on which you are lying. Your descendants will be like the dust of the earth, and you will spread out to

the west and to the east, to the north and to the south. All peoples on earth will be blessed through you and your offspring."

When I read that, I didn't get a clear understanding right away that God was talking to me about my future and what He was going to do with my life. I thought it was just for Jacob and his time. But the Bible is inspired by God, and the book of Timothy tells us that it is made useful for correcting, rebuking and thoroughly equipping the man of God for all good works (2 Timothy 3:16-17). God began to show me through this scripture that this was only the beginning of many visitations and visions that would take place in my life!

CHAPTER 4

Lord, Please Send Me an Angel!

In June of that same year, 1982, I returned to Philadelphia after finishing my second year at the Bible college. I wanted to work with my home church and be a blessing to them because they had taken on themselves the responsibility of paying my school tuition. I began going out on the streets, preaching on every street corner I could find. I continued to have powerful experiences in the spirit world. For example, I would look at people and see the sadness in their hearts even though they were well-dressed and looked prosperous.

However, living with my family became difficult for me. They weren't serving God, and this didn't help me at all. I noticed that I was becoming cold spiritually and was having thoughts of going back to my old way of life. The Holy Spirit continued to remind me how terrible my life would have been without God. The fear of God was so present in my life that I began to cry out to Him, saying, "God, I know you have a purpose for my life. I don't understand much of it. You have given me bits and pieces of it through dreams. I believe you are showing me that you have assigned angels to my life—I've seen how you have protected me wherever I have gone!"

Spiritual Darkness

One day while sitting on the porch of my oldest sister, Evelyn's house, I heard a shot. I saw Nancy, the woman who lived next door, come out of the

28

house, smiled at me, shut the door and leave. Then I heard a man's voice as if he was mumbling. He tried to open the door but he could not get out because Nancy had put a lock on the porch's gate. The man began to scream for someone to call the police because he had been shot—Nancy had shot her husband in the leg. After the police took him away, I learned that he was the son of a pastor friend of mine whom God was using mightily in Philadelphia—Pastor Fuentes. This pastor helped me many times in my crusades.

Evelyn's house was filled with turmoil. Sometimes my brothers and sisters would visit and get drunk. There were always problems in the neighborhood. I felt as if I was being oppressed by evil forces when I was there, yet I was encouraged that God was with me and had sent His angels to watch over me.

One day I received a letter from a young woman who lived in Mayaguez on the island of Puerto Rico. I didn't know who she was, but she had obtained my address from one of my friends. In her letter, this young woman told me the story of what happened in one of my crusades in Puerto Rico. A young man from a wealthy family visited her church. He accepted the Lord that day when I gave the altar call. He was only nineteen years old, and his name was Ario Matos, Jr., the son of a man who owned a satellite business and a secular radio station on the island of Puerto Rico in the 1980s. When Ario accepted the Lord, he decided to make the station a Christian radio station and wanted me to give my testimony on the air.

I wrote this young woman telling her that I would pray about doing this, and if I felt it was God's will, I would return in about two months, around November, 1982. Meanwhile, I called my friend, Eliezer Espinosa, who led a Christian salsa group that used to travel with me, ministering in music in my crusades. I asked him if he could help me set up some more meetings for when I returned to Puerto Rico. He agreed to help me and started to line up several meetings. I also called another friend, Johnny Alvarado. Johnny was a good brother in the Lord, and I had become very close to him and his wife Cucusa. I felt as if they were more my family than my natural family because of the way they treated me as their brother in the Lord. Johnny told me I could come to the radio station he was working with—Radio Revelation—because he would also like to interview me.

Go to the Altar and Pray!

When I returned to Puerto Rico, I had several meetings and radio interviews lined up. My first meeting was at a Disciples of Christ Church located on a mountain. It seemed like the biggest mountain to me—it took almost forty-five minutes to go up it. I stayed with the pastor of the church, Toin Cardona, who was also a friend of mine. When Sunday arrived, I felt cold and empty inside. I felt spiritually drained because I had preached so much in Philadelphia and had been around my family whose turmoil brought me even lower spiritually. That Sunday morning at Toin Cardona's church, I went into a room where there were already fifteen to twenty people praying. I told the Lord, "I don't feel strong. I feel like I am ready to quit. I don't feel Your presence. I don't feel Your Spirit in my life. If You are going to use me in this island, if this is Your purpose for me to be here, fill me up again and let me receive a touch of Your Spirit."

As I prayed this, a young woman who was also praying spoke to me.

"Brother Joey, go to the altar and pray. The Lord said He will meet you there."

Another brother got up and told me the same thing. I went to the front of the altar where many people were already gathering. When I reached the altar, I stood with my hands lifted to heaven. Suddenly, I felt as if fire was going down my body. It was such a wonderful feeling, and as hard as it is to describe, it seemed as if I was being baptized with more of the Holy Spirit. As the Holy Spirit came upon me, I began to feel His presence and glory in my life. I could feel my body trembling, and I started to cry out in my spirit to God. The next thing I knew, everyone there was praising God and shouting to Him. You could feel His presence as if His *shekinah*—His glory—fell on us that morning. It felt as if God was giving us a divine visitation, letting us know that His presence was with us.

After this experience, I preached, and the Lord gave me a powerful word. I encouraged the church with the Word of God and asked them to keep me in their prayers. I shared with them some of the experiences I had back in Philadelphia—how people tried to harm me in the street meetings, but God always delivered me from them. They rejoiced, glorifying God as they heard how He could save a man from violence, crime, drugs, gangs, and use him to preach the Gospel. Their faith was strengthened as they continued to believe that God was present with them too.

I then went to other churches in the same area of Bayamon ministering to the people. As I preached in these churches, however, I experienced great opposition. My car would break down or a meeting would be cancelled. Sometimes I didn't have enough finances to get from one place to another. I believed God would take care of me. However, even though He was seeing me through these hardships, I began to become discouraged. I wondered if I was out of the will of God and if I needed to return to Philadelphia.

Putting out a Fleece Like Gideon

Before I returned to the other side of the island, I spent the night at Eliezer's house. I began to question why I was having thoughts regarding God wanting me to return to Philadelphia. When I was back there, I became drained and spiritually cold. I began to realize that those thoughts were not from God but from the enemy who was trying to get me out of God's perfect will. That night in Eliezer's house, I began to pray.

"God, I'm fighting confusion. I understand Your Word says the author of confusion is the devil. He's a liar and the father of all lies. I'm going to put out a fleece just like Your servant Gideon did when You told him to go out to war. He felt he was the least worthy and from the smallest tribe of Israel, but You used him to deliver Israel from their enemies. I'm going to put out a fleece asking You to confirm if this is Your trip— if this is Your doing—because I do not want to be out of Your will. God, this might sound crazy but the Bible does talk about Your angels—how they came and appeared to many of Your servants. Just as Abraham experienced when he was sitting near the great tree in the plains of Mamre in his country.

The two angels that were with You when You visited Abraham and which You sent down to Sodom and Gomorrah, brought out Lot and his family. These two angels appeared to Lot and delivered him out of the city. The people were so perverted that the angels sent blindness upon them, and they were able to deliver Lot from the destruction that You sent on those cities.

In Luke 1:26-28, Your Word speaks of a woman named Mary living in Nazareth, and how an angel came to tell her that she would be with child because she had found favor in the eyes of the Lord. Everything that the angel said to her, she believed, and it came to pass. Well, Lord, if this is true about angels, I want you to do the same for me. Send me an angel! He will confirm to me that it is Your will for me to be here on this island, and that You will open many more doors for me so that I can continue to do Your will. Help me not be of two different minds. I am trying to serve You, and I am fighting this enemy who is attacking my mind."

Monday morning I was on my way to the west side of the island to stay with some friends, Raul Concepcion and his family, who lived in Anasco. My meetings were to start on Tuesday, I was supposed to be on the radio Wednesday, and Thursday I was to preach in a church that seated around three thousand people. I had other meetings on Sunday morning and Sunday evening. I told the Lord if He didn't send me an angel by Sunday, I would take that as a sign that it was not His will for me to be in Puerto Rico, and I would buy a plane ticket to fly back to Philadelphia the following Monday. In my heart I strongly believed God was going to send me an angel.

I realize to some people this might sound crazy. I knew God sent angels to deliver me before I knew Him and now that I was living for Him. Since He had sent His angels to deliver me from those who tried to hurt me as I preached the Gospel, I believed in my heart that I would see angels.

Going to the radio station on Wednesday, my emotions were low. I was being attacked mentally. I had only been saved for three years, and I was still learning to tell the difference between the voice of God and the voice of the devil. The devil will always try to imitate God and make you believe that God is speaking to you—when he is the one putting thoughts in your mind. Even though I was feeling down, as I talked about the Lord and told the people what He had done for me and what He could do for them, my spirits rose. Once I started talking about Him, I didn't know how to shut up because I was so in love with the Lord. Only He was able to give me all the peace, joy, and happiness I had found. I was just like the woman in the parable of the lost coin. She cleaned her whole house looking for the coin that was lost, and now, she had found it. That was the way I felt. I found what I had always looked for in life—happiness and joy. It didn't come to me from my parents, a woman, or even money. It was the joy that only Jesus gives!

When I met with Ario Matos around nine that Wednesday morning, he explained to me how the interview would work. The interview began, we talked for about an hour—and the phones at the station began to ring without stopping. I saw how excited the people were who were answering the phones. They kept giving Ario the sign to tell him to continue with the interview because there were so many calls. They knew that this interview was having a powerful impact on the people who heard it.

The Lord Confirms His Word

When we were finally finished, I stepped out of the interview area, and one of the people working there told me some people were there to meet me. They were from a Catholic Charismatic Renewal Church—I had never heard of that denomination. I asked what they wanted with me and was told they wanted me to be the main speaker at a retreat they were having for nearly five hundred people. I met their twenty-four year old pastor, David Ruiz. He told me about the retreat and asked me if I would be interested in coming. I told him I would be glad to come and speak! I mentioned that someone would have to pick me up because I didn't have a car. They told me that wasn't a problem, and they would send someone for me.

After I finished speaking with them, another pastor waiting there invited me to come to his church. Since I didn't have any more days available that week, I asked him to give me his number and told him I would call him Monday. However, I thought if God didn't send me an angel between now and Sunday, I would be on my way to Philadelphia on Monday. If no angel came, I would know I had to leave the island because I didn't want to be out of the will of God.

When I got up on Thursday morning, I was once again very low in spirits. My concern was being in the will of God. I loved to talk about the Lord—I was enjoying everything that was happening in our meetings. But, I was feeling down because I thought I was out of God's perfect will. I couldn't understand what the Lord wanted to do with my life. That morning as I started to pray, I said, "Lord, I still believe even today that You will send me an angel. The church where I'm preaching holds about three thousand people. If it is Your will for me to preach there and You are going to send me an angel, I want You to fill this church as another sign to me. Please fill this church with three thousand people—many will give their lives to You.

"I also want You to send me a missionary to confirm that You are going to send me an angel. But Lord, this missionary cannot be from the cities of Anasco, Aguada, or Mayaguez. If the missionary comes from any of those cities, I will know that You did not send him to me. If he is from another city, I will know that You sent him to tell me about the angel that is to come to me."

When I arrived at the church that morning, there were only two hundred people. I didn't realize, however, that this service was going to be broadcast live over the radio. After being handed the microphone to speak, I noticed that there were three microphones wrapped together with tape. I asked if the message was being transmitted live, and I was told, yes. When I saw the two hundred people, I realized that this was a Thursday at nine in the morning. Almost everyone was either at work or at school. Where were those three thousand people going to come from?

As I started to speak, sharing how the Lord had called me to Himself and to this ministry, I looked through the open windows of the church to see all of these cars pulling into the parking lot. While I continued to preach, the church continued to fill. It seemed as if all the people who lived nearby, that weren't in school or at work, had heard the message on the radio—and they wanted to come hear me in person! People even carried their bikes into church, putting them at the back before they sat down.

Healing the Sick and Casting out Demons

After I had spoken for almost an hour, the church was filled to capacity. I believe more than three thousand were there because I saw people standing at the back of the church and parents holding their children on their laps. When I saw the church was full, I began to feel much better about this trip, and I was convinced God would answer my prayer about the angel. Around fifty people responded to the altar call for salvation. As they came forward, I kept appealing for more people to give their lives to the Lord, for people in the church to come forward to receive prayer for healing and deliverance from tormenting spirits. When I said "tormenting spirits," I realized that I too had been tormented in my mind that whole week. I had constantly heard voices telling me that I was out of God's will, to leave the island, and that God wasn't with me.

Praying for the people who had come forward, I noticed a particular girl who was about nineteen years old. As I went to lay hands on her, I felt as if both my hands and feet were burning. This sensation went from the tip of my fingers to my elbows and from my feet to my knees. She started screaming loudly when my hands touched her. The voice that came from her was diabolic. She began twisting and sliding back and forth on the floor just like a snake. When I saw this, I grabbed her by the hand because she was being pulled away and dragged across the floor by those demonic powers. I commanded the powers of darkness, the spirits of evil, the demonic forces that had bound her to come out of her in the name of Jesus Christ. As soon as I said that, she screamed loudly, her body *elevated off the floor*, and suddenly, she was dropped back down again. A few seconds later, she began to weep.

The next thing I knew, she gave me a hug. I didn't understand what was going on, but I realized this girl had just been set free from the powers of darkness that had bound her. Upon praying for more people, I realized this girl was not the only one oppressed like this. There were around eight other people whom the Lord set free from bondage. Later on I discovered some of these people had been involved in witchcraft, spiritualism, and psychic activities. The people who came forward began to cry out to the Lord as they felt the presence of God and the infilling of the Spirit of God coming upon their lives. The people in the congregation were glorifying God, beseeching Him to do all that He wanted to do that day.

When the service was over, I was drenched with sweat! I saw nearly sixty men at the altar waiting to speak to me. Someone told me they were pastors who wanted me to come to their churches. They told me they wanted me to hold street meetings in their cities or minister in their churches. Some of them even wanted me to go to the prisons to preach the Word of God. Before I confirmed any engagements with them, I asked Brother Concepcion if it was all right to give them his phone number since I was staying with him and his family. He told me that was fine and gave the pastors his number. I told them to call me on Monday, and I would let them know when I could minister in their churches.

The Missionary With a Word

While speaking with the pastors, I kept noticing two other men standing to the side of the group. One of them was a pastor in Cabo Rojo. The other man standing next to him seemed to me to be a missionary because I noticed that his clothes didn't match! I kept watching him because he just stood there patiently, waiting for me to finish talking to the rest of the pastors. Once I finished giving them the information they needed, this strange-looking man walked up to me and said, "Brother Joey, I am a missionary. I have a word from the Lord to give you. I was listening to you on the radio, and the Lord told me to come to this church because He had a message for you concerning a petition you are praying about."

I asked him what city he was from, and he replied that he was from Moca. When he said that, I realized that he was not from the three cities I had mentioned to the Lord. Then I asked him what the message was he had for me from the Lord.

"Before I tell you the message, let me explain how I got here today. As I was listening to you, the Lord told me to come to this church to give you this message. I don't have a car. I walked three miles to the main highway. I stood there with my Bible in my hand. As I was standing there, I said to the Lord, 'God, if you want me to give this young man this message, then have someone stop and take me to this church.' As soon as I said that, this pastor who is standing next to me—Luis Troche—saw me and stopped. He asked me where I was going, and I told him I was going to Aguada, to the church where you were preaching. He told me he was coming here, too! Even though he was on his way home, he had decided to come to the church because he wanted to invite you to come preach in his church. He told me to get in his car, and here we are, standing in front of you!"

By this time, I was anxious to hear the message! I asked him again what the message was, and he said, "The Lord told me to tell you that this trip to the island of Puerto Rico is His doing. He brought you here for such a time as this. He is going to use you mightily. You have not seen anything yet. What He has done with you today is only a glimpse of what you will see in the near future. One thing that God wanted me to tell you is that you asked Him for a special petition. He didn't tell me what it was, but He did want me to tell you that you *will* see it."

When I heard that, I really became excited!

CHAPTER 5

God Sends Me an Angel!

I left the church that day with Brother Concepcion, his daughter Ivy, and his son Raul, Jr., and I was filled with excitement! In the car I began to tell them about the petition I had put before the Lord. I told them about the missionary and the things he told me. Then Brother Concepcion said, "I know you only asked to stay in my house for a week, but if God confirms this prayer request you have before Him and you need to stay longer, you can stay with us as long as you want. We will be delighted to have you. My children love to go to your meetings!" He had a beautiful family and told me that perhaps his son and daughters could help me minister in music because they were musicians. The next day, Friday, I had to minister in other churches. One of those churches was the one in which Ario Matos had been saved and the other church was pastored by Ismael Ramos who had heard me on another Christian radio station on the east side of the island.

I Wanted Sunday to Hurry Up!

I could hardly wait for the Thursday, Friday, and Saturday services to be over because I wanted Sunday to hurry up and get here! I wanted to see the angel that day. The Lord used me powerfully in the Thursday and Friday night services. Many people were saved, including several young people just coming in from the community who gave their hearts to the Lord. The Saturday morning service was at ten in the morning in the city of Isabella, about thirty minutes from Brother Concepcion's house. David Ruiz, the pastor of the church in Isabella, came to pick me up that morning. With him was Pastor David Aponte who pastored a Catholic Charismatic Renewal Church of about fifteen hundred members.

Pastor Aponte told me how his church had become a Catholic Charismatic Renewal Church. He had been filled with the Holy Spirit, and this caused him to leave his traditional Roman Catholic Church because the priest there did not want him teaching about the Holy Spirit. When we arrived in Isabella, I walked into the campground where the church was holding its retreat. About six hundred people were there that morning and after the worship, the service was turned over to me.

I'll just give my testimony quickly, I said to myself. After that, I'll give the altar call and pray for whoever comes forward. I wanted to hurry up and get the service finished because I wanted Sunday to get here! Being anxious to see Sunday, I was neglecting the other services in which I was ministering. All the pastors who asked me to come to their churches wanted me to share my life story. They wanted to hear how God had changed a criminal, a drug-dealer, a gang-leader. They wanted to hear how God called me by my name and how He was now using me for His glory.

As I shared my testimony, people began crying. My Spanish was so poor that it took about an hour and ten minutes just to give my testimony. I had been learning Spanish for the last three years, but it was still very rough. However, when I gave the altar call, about thirty-five to forty people came to the altar. When these people came forward, all I wanted to do was pray for them quickly and leave—I just wanted to get home. All I could think about was seeing the angel on Sunday.

A Greater Anointing for Ministry

However, as I began to pray for the people, the pastor took a microphone and began to challenge the people to give their hearts to the Lord. As he spoke, I opened my eyes again and there were at least twenty more people at the altar. Suddenly, I felt that burning in my hands again. I felt a healing anointing come upon me, and when I laid hands on one particular girl, she fell down and started to shout that she had been healed. This continued as I prayed for people that morning—people were getting healed from all sorts of ailments, and evil spirits were leaving some.

This particular morning there was also a girl who fell on the floor acting just like the girl who was delivered at the Pentecostal Church in Aguada. She was being pulled backwards, dragging herself toward the door at the back. I ran toward her and as I did, the anointing of God was so powerful upon me that people to my right and my left were being filled with the Spirit of God. When I finally reached this girl, I laid my right hand on her head and commanded the evil spirit to come out. She began to scream and it seemed as if there was a struggle, as if the spirit didn't want to leave her, but at the name of Jesus, he finally came out. After the screaming stopped, she began to weep. Before the spirit left her, her eyes had been very red, but now they were normal again. The peace of God was in her eyes.

After I prayed for another thirty minutes, people began to share with excitement what had happened to them—how the Lord had healed them from pain in their bodies and how their children had been set free. This brought such joy to my heart. It inspired me to learn even more of God and to see His will accomplished through my life! Remembering who I had once been in the past and now seeing what God was able to do through me by reaching so many people, I felt real joy.

When the service ended, I walked down the middle aisle of that chapel to where Raul Concepcion and his children were waiting to take me home with them. I was so hot and sweaty that I was terribly uncomfortable. As I walked out the door of the chapel, a twelve-year-old boy suddenly stood in front of me and placed his hand on my chest as if to tell me to stop.

"Brother Joey, stop a minute!"

He wouldn't let me out the door. When I looked at him, I noticed that there was something different, something very unusual about him. I knew that something tremendous had happened to him in the meeting. I thought the Lord had filled him with the Holy Spirit or perhaps he had experienced God's presence in a mighty way and wanted to tell me about it. He was holding a Bible open in his left hand, and I asked, "What is it you want to tell me?"

"There is a man over there who told me not to let you go until I give you this," he replied.

"His Hair Was Like Wool"

Standing and facing me, he took his right hand and pointed to his left side. I looked to see where he was pointing, but I didn't see anyone. On his other side, I saw Brother Raul, his son, his daughter, the pastor of the church, and a few other people. When Pastor Ruiz and Pastor Aponte saw this boy stop me, they came over to see what was going on. When the boy told me about the man standing there who had told him to give me the Scriptures to read, I thought, *Perhaps a demon came out of someone here and came into this boy, and now he is seeing things!*

While I said that to myself, the boy looked at me and with a voice of authority said, "Brother Joey, I rebuke those thoughts that you have in your mind right now! Those thoughts are of the devil!"

When I heard that, I became scared. I couldn't understand how this twelve-year-old boy knew what I was thinking.

"Joey, look!" he said again to me, and this time, he turned his whole body around with the Bible still open in his hand and pointed back toward the same place again.

"That man is still right there—he has not moved. He is dressed in white and has great wings coming out of his back. His hair is white like wool, and he has sandals on his feet. He is standing there right now!"

When the boy described this angel that he saw, I knew in my spirit that there was indeed someone there. I couldn't see him with my own eyes, but I knew he was standing there. I felt his presence. The boy turned around again, looking at me, and said,

45

"He told me to tell you that he is in all your crusades, and he will always be in all of your crusades the rest of your life."

When the people around us heard what the boy said, they began shouting to the Lord and praising His name. Even though none of us saw the angel, we all felt his presence. Finally, I asked the boy what the Lord had given me to read. He handed me his Bible, opened to Luke 9:1-6:

"When Jesus had called the twelve together, he gave them power and authority to drive out all demons and to cure diseases, and he sent them out to preach the kingdom of God and to heal the sick. He told them: "Take nothing for the journey— no staff, no bag, no bread, no money, no extra tunic. Whatever house you enter, stay there until you leave that town. If people do not welcome you, shake the dust off your feet when you leave their town, as a testimony against them." So they set out and went from village to village, preaching the gospel and healing people everywhere."

When I read this, I knew then that God sent me to the island. I personally did not see this angel, but knowing the experiences I had in Bible college in November of 1980, when I prayed early one morning, heard those wings flapping in the silence of the chapel and felt the presence of the angel there, I knew for a fact this boy had indeed seen the angel God had sent me. I went home so excited. Brother Raul was excited right along with me and told everyone what had happened in that service!

An Open Door of Utterance

From that day on, I started to book meetings throughout the entire island of Puerto Rico. I had only planned to be there for two weeks, but I ended up staying for almost six months. I was preaching every other day, and on occasion, I preached twice a day. Doors opened for me to go onto the campuses of universities.

The day I went to Central Catholic College of Bayamon, I was accompanied by Pastor Toin Cardona's son, Wilber, a high school teacher who spoke excellent English. He was the one responsible for getting me into the college to speak to the students and professors.

About fifteen professors and ninety students of psychology came to hear what I had to say. I wasn't allowed to talk about God, but they wanted to know about my background and my past. When I arrived, I began answering their questions concerning the criminal mind and about my being in gangs, hurting and even shooting people. After I spoke for about an hour, they asked me to tell them how I had changed—what had caused me to change.

I replied that if they wanted to hear the answer, it would take at least another half hour, and it would sound as if I was preaching because I would have to tell them exactly what happened to me. They agreed, and I began to relate how the Lord had called me. I told them how I had been ready to kill seventeen people, how I was planning to go into a police station and have a shoot-out with the police when I heard a voice that called me three times by my name. I told them that this voice explained to me why I had never been shot, stabbed, or killed during my entire violent life.

When I finished speaking to them, many of the students and even the professors were weeping. I didn't give an altar call because that was not allowed, but I knew that many were touched by the power of God. A few of the professors came to me and told me that what I had told in an hour and a half had taken them three semesters in college to learn. I replied that what they taught, they learned from books, but what I told them was what I had lived. I had experienced those things and knew the pain of my former life.

I was having even more success in my street preaching, and everywhere, I was ministering the Gospel of Jesus Christ. At times, I would feel a special anointing come upon me. Once when I was in Utuado, a local pastor, Porfilio, invited me to preach in his church. He had four sons—wonderful young men who loved the Lord. They asked me to preach even though their church didn't have that many members. I didn't care if they had five, ten—or ten thousand! I just wanted to talk about the Lord!

They took me from their town of Utuado to a small community (*barrio*) called Judas. Pastor Porfilio told me that he wanted to show me something and took me to a mountain where there were nearly one hundred houses. As I went with him to visit some of the people in those houses, to invite them to the meetings we were holding Thursday through Sunday, I began to feel such pain in my heart for them. I had never seen anything like their situation in my life. These were just shacks that had dirt floors and roofs made of metal sheets with holes in them. They kept chickens, pigs, sheep, and other animals—this is how they fed their families. I hadn't realized that there were people still living in these conditions. I had seen so much prosperity in the island that I could not imagine that people still lived like this. My heart went out to them.

A Miracle Before My Eyes

About thirty people showed up for the meeting on Thursday night. Since my testimony was long, I had broken it into three parts which I preached on Thursday, Friday, and Saturday, and then I preached the Word on Sunday. I preached that Thursday night for about forty minutes and gave an altar call. About twelve people came forward, and as I was praying for them, I noticed a ten or eleven year old boy. When I went to pray for him and laid my hands on his head, I noticed he had a lump on it. I figured someone had hit him with a rock, and it was simply swollen up there. But when I prayed in the name of Jesus, the lump disappeared, and his head became normal. I didn't pay too much attention to that because there were more people who needed prayer. Many received the Lord as their Savior, were healed, or delivered.

The next night I shared again for around forty minutes and gave the altar call. There were about sixty people in the church, a larger crowd than the night before. A woman came up for prayer with a scarf wrapped around her neck—like the heavy ones we use for the wintertime. I thought that was odd because it was so hot on the island. Why would she have a heavy scarf around her neck? As I laid my hands on this woman's head to pray for her, she began to scream, saying that a fire was burning her.

She fell to the ground. I didn't know what was going on so I continued to pray for the others who had come forward for prayer.

Then I became aware that the deacons of the church had picked her up from the ground. When they did, she began to shout and scream. I thought she was being really rude in interrupting the prayer that was going on for others! I asked pastor Porfilio why this woman was interrupting the service—I was still praying for people. He told me to look at her. She had taken the scarf off her neck, and I saw something that looked like stretched skin sagging on her shoulder. I asked her why her skin was like that, and she told me her story.

Her son was the boy with the lump on his head for whom I had prayed the previous night. He came home and told her that the evangelist had prayed for him.

"You see," she continued, "He had an appointment this morning at the hospital because that was a tumor on his head. But when you prayed for him, the tumor disappeared. I took him to the doctors this morning, and they asked me what happened to the tumor. My son told the doctors he had gone to a revival the night before and an evangelist from Philadelphia had prayed for him.

"My son explained to them, 'When he laid his hand on me, I felt like fire was burning in my head—I felt something leave me.'"

I told his mother that when I was praying for him, I had felt the lump but simply thought it was swollen because he had been hit in the head with a rock. She explained that it had been a tumor, and the doctors had told her that he didn't have long to live.

Now the doctors were taking all kinds of x-rays trying to find out what happened to him.

"I've been at the hospital almost all day today with him because they cannot find anything wrong with his head!"

He Gives Men His Power

She began to shout and glorify God at this point. Then she told me that she had had a cancerous tumor on her neck and had been wearing that scarf to cover it up. Before she came to the service, she had knelt to pray in her house.

"God, I know that this evangelist has no power in himself because he is only a man—but I know that You give men Your power and You have used this evangelist to heal my son, so I am going to step out in faith and go to that crusade. If You heal me of this tumor on my neck, I will serve You for the rest of my life."

She continued, "When you gave the altar call, I came up praying. As soon as you laid hands on me, it was just like my son had described it. I felt this sensation of fire that started going through my body as if it was burning me—but it was a good feeling. I can't completely describe what I felt, but I knew at the time that something was happening. I felt something leave me, and my neck felt light again."

When she told her story, we all began rejoicing and glorifying God for the great things He had done that day. This was only the beginning of many signs and miracles that took place on the island of Puerto Rico as I kept preaching the Word of God!

CHAPTER 6

The Man With the Gallon of Water

Just before I was to return to Philadelphia in June of 1982, I was invited to speak at a two-day crusade in the city of Canovanas at the El Tabor Church pastored by Juan Torres. Pastor Torres invited me because he heard me on the radio and he wanted me to hold a crusade at the baseball field in Canovanas. He had about one thousand people in his church, and he was expecting another two thousand to come to the crusade because they invited other churches to attend.

A Reason for a Break Down

I took Highway One that Sunday morning on my way from Mayaguez, on the west side of the island, to Canovanas. For no apparent reason, the engine started to emit smoke! A few minutes later, the engine was overheated, so I pulled to the side of the road to find out what was going on. There was hardly any traffic on the highway. When I opened the hood of the car, I saw something very odd. I couldn't understand how the dipstick that goes in the motor oil had somehow become loose and was now sitting on top of the motor! The radiator cap was also loose—as if someone had done this on purpose. I had no idea what was going on. All I knew was that the engine had overheated, and oil was leaking out because the dipstick wasn't in place!

There was no one around. Once in a while, a car would drive by, but, of course, no one stopped to help me. I was just standing there wondering what I was going to do next. I borrowed the car from my mother's husband—they were living on the island for some time now, and her husband knew I needed a car to get around.

I looked in the trunk to find some extra oil or a container of water. Thank God, I found some bottles of oil there! In my heart I felt this was not a coincidence but I was still puzzled as to how the dipstick had come out of the engine. Before I left Mayaguez, I had checked the engine, and everything was fine. Now, I was having problems that seemed to appear from nowhere! I looked down the road again to see if any cars were coming, but instead, I saw an enormous tractor-trailer truck coming down the highway. What really attracted my attention was that the driver was doing something terribly dangerous—I don't know how he managed it, but he had the driver's side door opened, and he was standing *outside the door*. He wasn't touching the wheel or the brakes.

"This guy is going to get himself or someone else killed driving like that," I thought to myself.

The Man with the Gallon of Water

Later on I found out there had been a major accident down the road. If my car had not overheated the way it did, I would most likely have been involved in it. I sat by the side of the road for about ten minutes as people drove by. I began to look around and saw mountains everywhere and heard the sound of water. I looked around only to see a stream of water coming out of the mountain. I was amazed because everything else was dried up. When I saw the water, I tried to find something to scoop it up with. I found four little bottles that someone had thrown to the side of the road. I picked them up and filled them with water. I had to make several trips to the stream because the bottles were so tiny. While I was pouring the water into the radiator after my third trip to the stream, I heard someone come up behind me.

When I turned around, I saw a man standing there with a whole gallon of water. He was wearing a tie, his face was glowing, and he had a big smile. I stared at him, wondering where he had come from because I hadn't seen or heard a car drive by me. When I looked at the car he was driving, there was another man in it. They looked like a pair of twins as they smiled at me.

The man standing in front of me handed me the gallon jug of water as I asked, "Don't I know you from somewhere?"

He smiled and said, "No."

"Are you a Christian?" I asked.

Once again, he smiled and said, "No," turning to walk toward his car. I was terribly puzzled as to where they had come from. I looked at the gallon of water and called out again, "Look, are you *sure* you're not a Christian?"

He smiled once more and said, "No," as he got into his car.

I turned around and began to pour the water into the radiator. When I finally drove away, I was still confused.

"Where have I seen this guy before?"

I *knew* that I had seen him somewhere—there was something different about him. I didn't know that later on in my walk with the Lord, I would see him again!

I finally reached Canovanas, and as I was getting ready to conduct this two-day crusade, I began to experience all sorts of opposition. I had sleepless nights where I would be up at two in the morning because demonic spirits were tormenting me. I'd get up to pray. I continued to rebuke these spirits in the name of Jesus, and great peace would enter my room, as if God Himself was present.

God Shows Himself Strong

On Tuesday, the first night of the crusade, God's presence was powerful. Around two hundred people were saved, and many people bound by witchcraft were being set free. Some of these witches came to the meeting to cast spells and release demonic powers upon me because they were upset that the Lord was using me to set people free from the devil. Then the second night as I was preaching, I could hear someone screaming out in the congregation. I couldn't see where it was coming from, but I noticed that everyone was looking over to my right. I turned to see what they were looking at, and I saw a woman running on the baseball field. No one was supposed to be on the field except the deacons and ushers from the church.

This woman was around twenty-five years old. I noticed that she had something shiny in her hands, but I couldn't tell what it was. She continued to run toward me, screaming at the top of her lungs. Drawing nearer, I noticed that she had a knife in each hand. When she was about three hundred feet away,

I told the people not to be worried. I turned and pointed at her.

"In the name of Jesus, devil, you come out of her!"

The moment I said that—and I am not exaggerating—this woman must have lifted up four feet from the ground and just flew back! She landed on her back and lay there with her arms up in the air, motionless. She looked as if she was paralyzed. I continued to preach as if nothing had happened.

After giving the altar call, I prayed with people to be saved and to be delivered. Pastor Juan came over to me and said, "Joey, the woman who was running toward you with the knives is still lying on the ground paralyzed! There are people over there praying for her—can you go find out what's going on?"

I went to where she was lying and noticed that she couldn't move. Her eyes were open, however, and there was an evil presence in them. The whites of her eyes had turned red. She was breathing as heavily as if smoke was coming out of her nostrils, and she still had the knives in her hands. I told someone to take them away, but even after the knives were gone, she still had her arms up in the air. I laid my hands on her and said, "In the name of Jesus, you evil spirits come out of her right now! I command you in the name of Jesus to set her free."

When I said that, I heard her scream loudly— and something came out of her! Then she sat up on the ground and sobbed. She began to tell everyone around her how miserable she had been, of the anger and hatred in her heart. That was why she had put spells on people and hated preachers. Even though she had been bound by spirits of witchcraft, she was set free that night by God's mercy and grace. She asked the Lord to forgive her for all the evil she had done and to remove the bitterness from her heart.

Return to Philadelphia

Despite seeing her mighty deliverance, encountering the two men who had helped me on the way to Canovanas, and watching how mightily God was moving in these two meetings, it was time for me to return to Philadelphia. I didn't know where I would live when I arrived so I called my youngest brother to see if he would let me stay with him. He said I could, and once I was there, I set about trying to find God's will for my life now that I was back in my hometown.

I was soon told about a job opening in the Lansdale-Telford area of Pennsylvania. I took the job and the opportunity it gave me to move out of the city. After living there for about six months, I realized that nothing was working right for me. I was in a car accident, which landed me in the hospital for three days. The streets had been covered in ice and snow, and I slid on the road and hit a telephone pole. I began to think that perhaps I was out of the will of God and that this was *not* where He wanted me to be. I felt out of place even though I was trying to adjust to the area.

Around that time, however, I met Damaris—the woman who was to become my wife. After dating her for close to a year, I received a phone call from Edwin Martinez, a pastor who was a friend of mine. He called to tell me that the Lord told him to contact me. He told me that God wanted him to work with me in ministry—to be a help to me. Oh, did that make me happy! I began to share with Edwin the vision the Lord gave me and the things He was telling me to do in the future.

"Joey, come over to my house tonight so we can talk some more about these things you are sharing with me!"

Speaking the Vision From God

I told him I'd be there around six in the evening with my girlfriend, Damaris, and my cousin, Edwin Perez. I waited for Edwin and Damaris to get off work and went to pick them up. We drove to Camden, New Jersey, where Edwin was living. His wife made dinner for us and afterwards, we sat down together. I began to share the vision the Lord gave me three years earlier. I told him about a building the Lord had shown me and about the people I saw working for the ministry. I also told him about the angelic visitations and how I believed God was going to do great things with me in the future. I explained that I believed God was going to bring people to the ministry who would be of tremendous help.

As I shared, I could see in Edwin and his wife's eyes that they thought I was crazy! Even my cousin and Damaris looked at me as if they wondered whether or not these things could come to pass.

"Man!" Edwin Martinez said at last, "That is a tremendous vision! If that ever comes to pass, then God is indeed powerful. Joey, whatever you do, when you get to that point, remember me."

"Pastor Edwin," I replied, "I'm here because you said God told you to work with me to get this vision off the ground. That means when I 'get there,' you will be right beside me!"

"Joey, you really have to have great faith to believe that!"

I reminded Pastor Edwin that nothing was impossible with God. It was starting to get late, and I told him that both Damaris and my cousin had to go to work the next morning, and I had an hour and a half drive back home.

"But before we leave, let's pray that God will fulfill the vision He has given me."

We took hands forming a circle and began to pray a simple prayer, but as we did, something began to happen to me. The only way I can describe it is to quote the Apostle Paul in II Corinthians 12:1-2:

> **"I must go on boasting. Although there is nothing to be gained, I will go on to visions and revelations from the Lord. I know a man in Christ who fourteen years ago was caught up to the third heaven. Whether it was in the body or out of the body I do not know—God knows."**

I say the same thing along with Paul because that night as we prayed, I felt my body become cold and begin to jerk. When this happened, whether I was "in the body or in the spirit," I don't know, but as Paul said, "God knows!" When I opened my eyes, I found myself back in Philadelphia, standing on the corner of 3rd and Somerset Streets. It was daytime, very bright outside. But as I was standing on that corner, everything became dark, and I could see demonic forces-spirits flying all over the city. They would come down to people to torment them. As I watched, I heard a voice say to me, "Look and observe what you see." I kept looking, and I saw people—but I could also see evil spirits inside of them tormenting them. When I looked down the street, I saw a bar with many people just hanging out there. I saw the spirits descend and go into people and then they would fly back upwards. The whole city was darkened by the power of the devil.

Clearing the Atmosphere of the Enemy's Forces

Suddenly, I looked and right in front of me, I saw an angel about seven feet off the ground. His hair seemed like clouds, and he had a strap around his head. Enormous wings came out of his back, and he was dressed in white with sandals on his feet. In his right hand, he held a sword. He must have been about six or seven feet tall—he was much larger than I was! He took a step forward and swung the sword he held. All I could hear was that sword cutting through the air, making a whistling sound. As it descended, the demonic spirits in the air were scattered left and right.

Then the angel took a second step forward, swinging his sword again. I could see the spirits scattered even more, leaving the air clear of their presence. Every time the angel would swing his sword, I could hear that whistling sound, like the wind of a hurricane. He swung the sword a third and a fourth and a fifth time—and the air was completely clean. Everything looked bright again—I could see white clouds and blue sky. There were no more evil spirits in the air. As that sword descended each time, breaking through the forces of evil, I could see the doors being opened to the vision God had given me.

The angel stopped swinging his sword, turned, and looked at me. He took the sword in his hand and held it in front of himself with the point downward. He was still standing in the air, and with both hands he gripped the hilt of that sword. He stared at me as I looked back at him, and his face and clothes seemed to be almost fluorescent as they glowed. It was just like in the Bible when Mary Magdalene and Mary the mother of James went to the tomb to look for Jesus. They saw two angels who were gleaming and whose clothes were shining.

Looking at me, he pointed at me with his right hand and spoke.

"The way you believe is the way I'll move. But the moment you stop praying, the moment you stop seeking, and the moment you stop believing, I'll stop, and I'll wait on you."

As soon as he said "I'll stop, and I'll wait on you," I found myself back in Camden, New Jersey.

"Man, your hands got cold," my cousin Edwin told me. "It looked like you weren't really there!"

Damaris said the same thing, and I told them what had happened.

"I don't know how to explain this to you. Even though my body was here, my spirit was in Philadelphia. I was standing on a corner, and I saw an angel with a sword. He swung this sword five times. Every time he did, he cleared the sky of demonic forces, and I saw the doors opened to the future of the vision God has given me!"

After I told them that, we ended up staying another forty-five minutes, praising and glorifying God because His power had fallen on Pastor Edwin's house. I was tremendously excited after this experience! I dropped off my cousin Edwin and Damaris and drove home to Telford where I was staying. I could still feel the presence and anointing of God in my life. Meditating on what happened while I drove home, I was overwhelmed with joy because of my experience with the angel.

That night I couldn't sleep. I tossed and turned because I still felt the excitement of that experience. I got up at about five thirty in the morning to pray. I spent about forty-five minutes praying for the lost, the poor, the homeless, and for those bound by drug addiction and prostitution. Then I prayed for the young people and gave God the glory for all He was doing. After about an hour and a half, I fell silent. As I was quiet before the Lord, the Holy Spirit told me to read Matthew 8-11. Then He told me to read Hebrews 1 and Habbakuk 2. I had studied the book of Habbakuk in Bible college, but it had never been a book that caught my attention. I read these chapters in Matthew and Hebrews before and couldn't understand why the Lord wanted me to read them again.

His Word Instructs Me Concerning His Angels

However, as I read verse 14 of Hebrews 1, I knew what was going on. Hebrews 1:14 says "Are not all angels ministering spirits sent to serve those who will inherit salvation?" As soon as I read that, I knew that God was confirming that angels had been assigned to me by His mighty power to protect me and guide me into my purpose and destiny in Christ. Then, I read Habbakuk 2:2-3:

"Then the Lord replied: "Write down the revelation and make it plain on tablets so that a herald may run with it. For the revelation awaits an appointed time; it speaks of the end and will not prove false. Though it linger, wait for it; it will certainly come and will not delay."

When I read this, I knew for a fact that I was supposed to write the vision down on paper so that I could explain it to people. I needed to know exactly what God wanted me to do in this vision and to bring it forth plainly so that others might understand it as well.

In Matthew 8-11, Jesus spoke of the faith the centurion had and how he believed. He talked about the man with leprosy and how he, too, believed God. Then, I read about the woman with the issue of blood and how she had reached out and touched Jesus in faith. As I continued to read, I saw how He healed people and set them free, casting demons out of some. What touched me the most about all these things I read in the Bible was the way these people believed in God. The centurion believed that Jesus only had to say the word, and his servant would be healed. The woman with the issue of blood believed if she could only touch the hem of Jesus' garment, she would be made whole. As I read, my mind went back to the experience the night before.

That night, April 8th, in Camden, New Jersey, the angel appeared to me and said that according to the way I believed, he would move on my behalf. The moment I stopped seeking, believing, or praying, he would stop and wait on me.

I knew I had a task to accomplish—a job to do for the glory of God. The Lord had assigned angels to me, and they would move on my behalf as I continued to trust and believe His Word. But that meant I had to *take* Him at His Word. I looked up the word "believe" because I wanted to make sure I understood its meaning. I found that it means "to take a statement or a promise of a person to be true or real." When I read this, I understood if I was going to believe the Lord, I would have to take His "statement"—which is His Word and the words of the angel—as true and real. God's Son, Jesus Christ, is true and real. God Himself is true and real. I had to believe what He said!

CHAPTER 7

I Saw My Angel

I was now a man on fire! I began to read the Gospels over and over. I wanted to learn about Jesus and how He ministered. The more I read and studied His Word, the more my faith increased to believe Him. As I read in the Scriptures of people who came to Christ unable to walk, I saw that they made an effort, believing that He could perform a miracle in their lives. I read in the Gospels where four men took their friend who could not walk, climbed onto a roof where Jesus was teaching, cut a hole in it, and lowered him to where Jesus was. Jesus told them that because of their faith, the man was healed.

I knew believing God's Word would produce results as I trusted Him to perform what He said He would in my life. The more I spoke about the vision—the more I spoke about the goodness and power of God—the more I saw that vision becoming real in my own life.

The Vision Will Come to Pass

One day I sat with my friend Lance Walnou and his wife Anabel, sharing the vision and my experience with the angel. I told him of other experiences with angels that I had in Bible college. As I spoke, I saw that look in Lance's eyes which said, "This guy has *got* to be crazy!" But when I went back to see him again and continued to share the vision and my experiences with some of his friends, Lance looked at me with belief and said, "You really believe this vision."

"Yes, I do, Lance, because *God* gave me this vision."

"Joey, I don't doubt that it will come to pass because you believe it so strongly."

Lance introduced me to his pastors, the Reverend Ron Breaux and his wife Jean, who were pastoring the Church of Acts in Ambler, Pennsylvania. I met with Pastor Ron and began to share with him the vision God had given me and what I believe God was going to do with my life. He was touched by what I told him.

"Joey, I want to be a part of what you are doing. I want to help you in every way we can through our church."

I told him about the Thanksgiving dinners we were planning to feed the poor and the homeless. He began to encourage his church to get involved. They started donating turkeys and cooking them. Later on, I became a member of his church because of his words of wisdom and encouragement. I believe Pastor Breaux was a powerful, anointed man of God who had a strong prophetic anointing and believed in healing and deliverance. I saw the way God used him in these gifts, as well as, in the gifts of the word of knowledge and discernment.

He traveled with me to the Dominican Republic and Puerto Rico where the Lord used him powerfully. In addition to the help he had already given me, he also backed us up by coming to the street meetings we held in north, south, and west Philadelphia. He didn't have a big church, but at least forty percent of his members came to the meetings to support us.

They were involved in everything we did—passing out flyers and tracts, feeding people and handing out clothes.

Delivered from the Violence

I held a street meeting on the corner of Hancock and Cambria Streets in north Philadelphia. Pastor Breaux and many of his church members came to the city to assist us. I brought Eliezer Espinosa and his orchestra from Puerto Rico to help us with the music. They played Hispanic Christian music, especially salsa. Many unbelievers were standing on the corners listening to what was going on. As Pastor Breaux and I stood on opposite corners of Hancock and Cambria, I noticed a large group of people who had gathered there. When I walked over to Damaris, now my wife and expecting our first daughter Christine, I felt Jesus' presence as if He poured something on me. Then I heard these words: "You are covered by the blood." I was wondering why the Lord said this to me as I spoke with Pastor Breaux. Just then, looking down the street facing east, I saw a Hispanic man who ran up to another man with a gun in his hand. I heard a shout—and standing only one hundred feet away from me, this Hispanic man shot a man in the neck who had been standing on the corner listening to Eliezer's orchestra.

The man who had been shot lay on the ground with a big hole in the side of his neck. Pastor Breaux and I went to him and took his hands. I saw that his eyes were beginning to roll back into his head and that he was about to die.

"You don't know me, and I don't know you. But if you die right now in your sins, you will go to hell—and that's not what God wants for you. He wants to set you free right now and give you this opportunity to receive Jesus as your Savior. You could die right now, but at least you will be with the Lord. Do you want to receive Jesus as your Lord and Savior and repent of your sins?"

The man was able to talk and said, "Yes." I could hear the police and the ambulance sirens, so I asked him to repeat the sinner's prayer with me before they arrived. I asked if he understood what he was doing, and he said that he did. We began to pray with him. Then someone said that Richie, the second leader of the Midtown Zulu gang, the gang I had once led, was there also.

Richie ran up to me asking what had happened to his brother-in-law.

"Richie, is this man your brother-in-law? Someone shot him in the neck!"

Richie began to curse because he was so upset. I told him to calm down because his cursing wasn't going to help his brother-in-law. Right then, the ambulance and the police arrived and took him away. I found out later that Richie's brother-in-law lived another five days and then died. I realized that the voice that told me, "You're covered by the blood," was the Lord letting me know that it didn't matter where I went in these violent communities, I would always be covered by the blood of the Lamb, Jesus Christ, and be protected.

When You Least Expect It

The next time I preached, I entitled my message "Death will walk up on you when you least expect it." I spoke for about twenty-five minutes with a godly anger because the enemy had tried to take the life of this young man. Thank God we were able to get to him and tell him about Jesus. By His grace and mercy, Richie's brother-in-law was able to remain conscious long enough to make that decision to receive Jesus as Lord. As I gave the altar call, I reminded everyone that death could come up on them when they least expected it, but they had an opportunity to change their lives by receiving Jesus. Many people, at least thirty, came to the altar that night. Some of them had been my friends in the past—men and women who had once bought drugs from me. Some of them hugged me, telling me to keep up the good work.

We spent the rest of the summer holding more street meetings in Philadelphia and other areas in the Northeast of the United States. Pastor George Bojorquez of Victory Outreach Ministry in Newark, New Jersey, invited me to do a street meeting there. He heard about me from another friend of his, Pastor Thomas Espinosa who was also from Victory Outreach Ministry and had started a church in Philadelphia. I had helped Pastor Espinosa with some street meetings and directed the people who had been saved to go to his church for follow up.

By the time we went to Newark, New Jersey, to work with Pastor Bojorquez, Damaris was about six months pregnant—and we were going into some violent projects. People told me this place was known as the "bad lands." Drug dealers came to tell me they had a couple of guys with rifles nearby, and they were aiming them at us! If we didn't get out of their neighborhood, they were going to start shooting. I looked around the area and could see guys in the windows with rifles pointed in our direction. At first I felt intimidated by this threat, but then the presence of God came upon me, and the peace of God reminded me that "I have given you power and authority to bind the forces of evil and to drive out evil spirits."

I told Pastor Bojorquez and the drug dealers, "We are not leaving. Right now, in the name of Jesus, we're doing a street meeting here whether you like it or not and you're not going to shoot anyone here today! You need to listen to this message." I was able to share with those drug dealers that there was hope in Jesus, and I asked them if they wanted to change their lives. They just laughed and walked away.

The Angels Bring Freedom to Minister

We set up the sound equipment and a flat-bed stage on wheels that we hauled around in our van. As I started to speak, I could feel the strong forces of evil in this community. I didn't feel "free" in my preaching, it was as if I was fighting a force beyond my control. I told the people from the church to start praying. We began to bind those demonic forces, breaking generational curses and the spirits of addiction and sorcery in the name of the Lord. As we prayed, I asked the Lord to assign angels to us and to have them surround this place.

After praying, I felt in my spirit that the air became clean. I sensed such a peace when I continued to preach. The anointing and the boldness of God were so strong when I gave the altar call, between twenty and thirty people came to the altar. Even some of the men who had come to buy drugs accepted the Lord that night and got rid of their drugs that same day.

The next night we went to another project to hold a second meeting. We set our stage up across from the projects in front of a corner store. The owner of the store gave us permission to set up our equipment there because he had been having a number of problems in the area. He hoped that perhaps things would be better for him if we held the meeting. The projects consisted of three high-rise buildings, each about fourteen stories tall. I didn't have any money in my pocket. I hoped once these meetings were over, that the pastor would at least give us some offering to help us get back to Philadelphia.

"You're Not Cutting Anyone!"

We held three meetings in Newark, New Jersey, and when the last one was over, I suddenly wanted some juice to drink made from the *guanabana* fruit that grows on the island of Puerto Rico. I didn't know why I had that craving—maybe I was getting all the cravings instead of Damaris. I remember we had a big audience as I preached, and the people from the church testified. There were people looking out their apartment windows and people sitting on a little platform around the building. There were also people standing on the other three corners of the intersection, listening to the Word of God. Some people had parked their cars to listen. When I gave the altar call, around twelve people came forward for salvation. One woman came forward with a knife in each hand. She walked up to me with no shame or fear and said, "If God can really change you, then I am going to give Him a chance. Preacher, if God does not change me today, I'm going to cut you all up, right now!"

Across the street, there were some guys who started to laugh, encouraging her to cut me up. I could see in her eyes that she was full of anger and hurt. She seemed to hate everyone. She was a stocky woman, and I could tell she had had a rough life.

"Woman, in the name of Jesus, you're not cutting anyone!"

As soon as I said that and laid hands on her, she fell to the ground and began screaming. Everyone become quiet. Even those guys who were laughing fell silent. I continued to pray for her, commanding all the forces of evil that bound her to come out. She continued to scream. Suddenly, she started to cry. When she got up from the ground, she hugged me and all the people on my team. I went on to pray for the rest of those who came forward, and as I did, they fell to the ground under the power of God. They began to cry in such pain. When I looked around, there must have been nearly fifty people at the altar. When I finally finished praying for them, I turned the service over to Pastor Bojorquez. I was standing about ten feet from him, and Damaris was about seven feet from me on my right. My ex-brother-in-law, whom I called "Baby Smoky Robinson" because he traveled with us as a soloist and sounded just like the great Motown singer, began breaking down the sound equipment.

A Glass of Juice

As I stood there, a man came up to me out of nowhere and put his right arm around my shoulder.

"Here, Joey!"

He gave me some *guanabana* juice.

"Where did you come from? You know, I've been wanting one of these juices for the past two days!"

"I know," he replied.

"You do?"

"Yes," he said, "I know."

I kept thinking to myself that I had seen this man somewhere before.

"Joey, you did a good job. I was with you yesterday. The Lord really used you. I'll see you tomorrow."

He walked away. I took just five steps, and John Valley saw me with the juice and asked me where I had gotten it.

"That guy over there gave it to me."

I turned around again, but I didn't see him. I walked about six or seven steps and looked around some more. When I still didn't see him, I asked Damaris, "Did you see that guy who came out of nowhere and gave me this juice?"

She said that she did. I asked if she knew where he had come from, but she didn't know. She just repeated that he had come "out of nowhere." When she said that, I told her that there was something strange about him. She replied that he did indeed look strange. I told her I knew I had see him somewhere before.

John came over to talk with us.

"Joey, what happened to the guy who was talking to you? It looked like he just disappeared!"

I told John I didn't know, and that was the end of it, or so I thought.

I Had Seen Him Before

The next day we held a street meeting in front of the Victory Outreach Church Center where they had a men's rehabilitation program. As we were setting up for the meeting, Damaris asked, "Joey, what's wrong with you? You look as if something is bothering you." I told her that it was nothing, that I was just fine. But she knew that something *was* bothering me and kept watching me. I kept looking around to see if I could see that man again because he had told me he would be in my next meeting. Suddenly, a sadness overwhelmed me because I *knew* I had seen this man before—and I wanted to ask him where.

He never showed up. That night, not too many people showed up, and only eight to twelve people responded to the altar call. I prayed for them, asking the Lord to bless them. While we were putting the sound equipment away, my wife came to me and asked, "Joey, are you okay? You look strange, as if something is bothering you." Once more, I told her I was fine.

"Joey, you've been kind of quiet—and that's not you! You're always talking."

She didn't know that I was still thinking about the man I saw the night before. After putting the sound equipment away, it was still early—about nine in the evening. We got on the New Jersey Turnpike to return to Philadelphia. When we had been in the van for about forty-five minutes, Damaris asked me once more if I was all right because I was just too quiet. At first I repeated that everything was fine, then I told her the truth.

"You know, something about the man I saw last night is still bothering me. I *know* I have seen him before, but I can't remember where."

Damaris and John both told me they thought there was something strange about him. No one could find him, and he had disappeared so fast. I told her I had been looking for him that night, but he didn't show up. As soon as I said that, I felt the presence of God come into the van. John and Damaris felt His presence too. It was as if someone was pouring the river of living water into our bodies. Then I heard a voice in my spirit.

"He was there; you just didn't see him."

When I heard that, I repeated it to Damaris. Then the Lord reminded me—as clearly as possible—of the day I was on Highway One in Puerto Rico in 1982, on my way to Canovanas to preach when my car broke down. He reminded me of the two men who came out of nowhere and gave me a gallon of water.

"That's it! That's the same guy!"

I asked the Lord why he had said he wasn't a Christian when I had asked him that night on the road. The Lord reminded me that angels are not Christians. Only those who accept Jesus as their Savior are Christians. That's why the man with the gallon of water said he wasn't a Christian. *He was an angel sent by God to help me in that situation!*

Was I making this up? Are angels real? I know this story might sound crazy, but I had two or three witnesses who were there and saw this man give me the juice I had been craving. The Bible is clear: "Are not all angels ministering spirits sent to serve those who will inherit salvation?" I had seen an angel that God sent to minister to me. He gave me the water when my car broke down. He handed me juice that I was craving. He was an angel sent by God to minister to me. *Angels are real, and I had just seen one.*

CHAPTER 8

God Demonstrates His Power

After we finished the street meetings in Newark, New Jersey, I was invited to Passaic, New Jersey by Pastor Gomez to hold street meetings. He told me the problems he had with the young people and that drugs, violence, and murder were prevalent in that area. He asked me specifically if I would go to a particular area known for its violence. Even Christians wouldn't walk down those streets because of the high crime rate. I told him all the shooting and violence would not stop me from going to preach the gospel. I knew the Lord was with me, and I wasn't afraid to go with Him.

Arriving at a particular corner in Passaic, New Jersey, the air felt heavy and dark even though it was still daytime. As our group ministered in music, I began to sense the demonic presence in that area. While they sang, I could feel the tension in the air and noticed people gesturing for us to leave. They didn't want us there; people across the street cursed us. But our young people kept on ministering in song, and I started to pray, asking God to send His angels to the four corners of that neighborhood. I began to bind every force of evil, every power of darkness.

Power to Bind and Loose

The Bible reminds us that God has given us the power and authority to tread upon serpents and scorpions and to overcome all the power of the enemy. I wasn't going to let the profanity, the tension, the heaviness in the air put fear in my heart. However, I could tell that some of the Christians present were afraid. There must have been two to three hundred unsaved people on that corner. I continued to meditate on God's Word and bind the powers of darkness. Scripture tells us plainly that we have the keys to heaven, and whatever we bind on earth shall be bound in heaven. Whatever we loose on earth shall be loosed in heaven. The Bible also says that the gates of hell shall not prevail against His Church. It's not talking about a building—but about us, for we are the Church of Jesus Christ. We are the ones in whom Christ has placed His Holy Spirit so we can walk into these areas free from fear of harm. And if anyone should be intimidated, it should be those powers of darkness because of the presence of God living within us through His Son Jesus Christ and through the presence of His Holy Spirit.

I continued to pray, believing that God was going to work a miracle. I went to the pastor and told him to round up a group of people to pray.

"There is so much tension in the air. A bunch of those people are getting really loud, and they don't want us here. Get these people from your church and tell them to stand behind the stage praying. Tell them to bind the powers of darkness so that when I begin preaching, there will be a free atmosphere in which I can bring forth the Gospel."

As they turned to pray for me, I went to the altar and spoke to the crowd.

"I am from Philadelphia, and I have come to this community to preach the Gospel. Right now, in the name of Jesus, I bind every power of darkness, every principality, ruler, governor, and evil force in high places!"

When I said, "In the name of Jesus," I said it with such authority that the whole community became quiet. I began to share my life story, telling them that I hadn't been brought up in church. I hadn't been a Christian all my life. I explained how I had been a drug dealer and a gang leader in Philadelphia, how I committed crimes and destroyed families, homes, and people's lives. As I spoke, I watched the way people were listening. I could sense a great anointing and the presence of God in that place. I preached with such boldness and power that everyone was attentive.

When I finished, I told Aby—a young man from the church—to go to the altar and start playing the piano. I asked everyone to bow their heads, and I was surprised to see even the unsaved put their heads down. Earlier, these people cursed us, telling us they didn't want us there. They had wanted us to leave. But the presence of the Lord was so strong when I told them to bow their heads so I could pray for them, they did it. As I prayed, asking God to set these people free, to touch them, to heal them, to take the pain from their hearts, I noticed they became silent. When I gave the altar call, I spoke in both English and Spanish, and about twenty Hispanics who did not speak English came forward, and another twenty who understood English came to the altar too.

"I Want to Break Your Face!"

Then within a minute or so, about fifty people crowded around the altar. Leading them through a prayer of salvation, God's presence became even stronger. Suddenly a man came through the crowd with a cup in his hands. I could tell he was drunk. He was a husky man, and he walked right up to me.

"You know what, Preacher? Right now I feel like breaking your face!"

"Why," I asked, "do you want to do that?"

"I just feel like breaking your face," he replied. "I don't like you!"

I looked into his red eyes and could see the powers of darkness inside him. Once more, holding the cup of whisky in his hand, with his breath smelling of liquor, he tried to intimidate me, telling me he wanted to hit me. My first instinct was to get into position just in case he decided to take a swing at me so I could punch him out. I was in a stance ready to defend myself when I felt the presence and the peace of God. That presence told me not to be afraid of this man.

Two other men who looked like body-builders came over to me.

"Preacher, do you want us to take care of this guy for you?"

"No," I told them, "I can handle him."

I looked at the man and told him, "You had better not lay a hand on me because if you try to hurt me, I will defend myself. And in the name of Jesus, I bind every power of darkness in you."

At that, the man began to laugh diabolically and walk away. Once again the two body-builders asked, "Preacher, do you want us to take care of this guy for you?"

I told them no, and they walked away. Then a Hispanic man came up to me with a little boy in a wheel chair. His son had been born crippled.

The Angels Battled for Me

"This boy has something to tell you!"

I asked him what he wanted to say, and the boy said, "You know, Joey"—he knew who I was because I had told the crowd my name as I was preaching—"When you were preaching, I was watching for a while, and I thought I was seeing things. As you were preaching at the altar, there were two angels with wings, dressed in white standing on your right and on your left. They just stood there smiling as you preached.

"I could see a battle in the air. There were spirits like shadows in the air, and then I saw angels fighting them. However, the two angels on either side of you didn't move. They stood there the whole time you were preaching. I noticed more angels came and started to chase away all the shadows in the air. I thought I was seeing things!"

"You weren't seeing things," I told him. "What you saw was real. This is not the first time I have heard this. You saw what God allowed you to see because He wanted me to hear it."

That day, I knew my prayers had been answered. The prayers of the people praying behind the altar had been answered. Because they had prayed, the angels of God were moving on our behalf. They were cleaning up the air, binding the powers of darkness.

Angels are real! Psalm 103 tells us, "Praise the Lord, you His angels, you mighty ones who do His bidding, who obey His Word. Praise the Lord, all His heavenly hosts, you His servants who do His will."

Angels have been assigned to us to help and protect us. When we call on God and ask Him to send His angels to us, they come. When we pray to God in faith, they move on our behalf. That's why the air had become so clean, and there was such peace as I was preaching. When I prayed that first prayer and asked the Lord to bind all the powers of darkness and assign His angels to the four corners of that community in the name of Jesus, He did just that.

God's Word Concerning Angels

The Bible speaks a great deal about angels. It tells of the prayers of the saints, and the way in which God moves on behalf of His people. In Matthew 4, Jesus was guided by the Spirit of God to go out into the wilderness to be tempted by the devil. At times it felt as if God had called me to go to the threshold of hell and to the den of iniquity where the powers of darkness ruled, controlling people who lived lives of sin. In Matthew 4:4, Jesus answered the devil, saying, "It is written: Man does not live on bread alone, but on every word that comes from the mouth of God." This passage continues, "Then the devil took Him to the holy city and had Him stand on the highest point of the temple. 'If You are the Son of God,' he said, 'throw yourself down. For it is written: He will command His angels concerning You, and they will lift You up in their hands, so that You will not strike Your foot against a stone.'" Here we see how Satan himself quoted the Scriptures trying to get Jesus to do what was contrary to God's Word.

This passage continues in verses 7 through 11:

"It is also written: Do not put the Lord your God to the test." Again, the devil took him to a very high mountain and showed him all the kingdoms of the world and their splendor. He said, "All this I will give you if you will bow down and worship me." Jesus said to him, "Away from me, Satan! For it is written: Worship the Lord your God, and serve Him only." Then the devil left Him, and angels came and attended Him."**

Here we see that when we are doing the will of God, when we are walking in His presence, obedient to Him, the angels move on our behalf. When we bind the powers of darkness in the name of Jesus Christ, the angels of God work for us. They begin to make a way for the purpose and calling of God to go forth in our lives. I knew the Lord called me into these dangerous, violent areas, and I also knew that through His angels, He gave me a hedge of protection. I could go where He led me with no fear of what might happen.

The Angels Are Your Hedge of Protection

My brothers and sisters, you too, have that hedge of protection. You have the Lord Jesus Christ, and you have His powerful angels to fight the forces of evil that we cannot see or understand!

The next evening the church prayed as we were setting up the equipment, and the whole atmosphere changed. The peace of God came upon that corner, and the people were even more attentive than they had been the night before. They wanted to hear the Word of God. I preached a bilingual message, translating the message from English to Spanish as I went along. When I gave the altar call, the young man who had threatened the night before to punch me in the face came forward crying. He hugged me and even kissed me on the cheek, asking my forgiveness for what he had done. He told me how grateful he was to God for bringing us there to give him the message of salvation. He shared with me the hatred, anger, and bitterness that had filled his heart, opening up about the pain in his life.

When people saw this, they flooded the altar. Once more, you could feel God's presence and power. I didn't have to see the angels on the altar to know they were there. The boy who told me the night before about the angels came up to me again. This time he said he didn't see anything. I still knew they were there. When we finished those street meetings in the summer of 1988, I praised God for those experiences in which He showed himself faithful and powerful, protecting us from danger.

CHAPTER 9

The Enemy Strikes Back

On March 4, 1989, my first daughter, Christine Lynette, was born. I was so excited God had blessed me with a child. When she was five months old in August of 1989, we took her with us to the street meetings. I would carry her up on the stage with me. After preaching, I looked forward to spending time with her, hugging and kissing my baby daughter. I was so very happy with my little girl and wanted her to be part of what God was doing through our lives in our street meetings.

One of my good friends, Pastor Ron Parks, caught the vision we had for the streets. For about four years, from 1987-1990, he worked with us every summer at the street meetings in the Philadelphia area. He rented a church building on the corner of 27th and Wharton Streets, and he wanted me to do a street meeting in that area. I invited my pastor from when I lived in Telford—Pastor John Yamin who had a church in Quakertown, Pennsylvania—and asked him if he would help train the people doing street meetings. He and two elders from his church, David Berry and Terry Moore, came to Philadelphia to work with people who shared the same vision for street meetings. About three hundred people came out to the training including fifty to sixty pastors who wanted to conduct street meetings in their areas.

"Get Out of My Community!"

The summer of 1989, we scheduled meetings from May to September in Philadelphia. Pastor John Yamin sent out a team of fifteen people along with volunteers from other churches to pass out flyers and tracts in the community. We served barbeque chicken and hot dogs at the meetings, and thanks to a monthly offering from Operation Blessing—700 Club, we were able to give groceries to those in need. Since they were the ones sponsoring the grocery giveaway, we put their labels on the grocery bags to let people know that it was Operation Blessing who had blessed them with food.

We also gave out clothing to people. Two members of Pastor Yamin's church went door to door passing out flyers, and something strange happened when they did this. They came to the home of a woman who was about sixty years old but who looked much older. She appeared miserable and full of anger—and she was very drunk! She was wearing a wig, but it was falling off her head. She was African-American, and when these two white men knocked on her door, she cursed at them, asking, "Why do you come knocking on my door? Get out of my community—I don't want you here."

Those two men simply stood there demonstrating the love of Jesus and telling her about Him.

"We just came to tell you about this Puerto Rican man who is going to be preaching on the corner—he is going to talk about a Jew whose name is Jesus. If you go, Jesus will give you peace in your life!"

She calmed down and told them that she couldn't walk that far.

"Next week I'm going to the hospital because I have gangrene in my right leg—I'm afraid the doctors will have to amputate it."

They understood why she was so miserable—that's why she tried to drink her problems away. But they also told her that with God, nothing is impossible—if she would come to the meeting and ask for prayer, God would heal her. She told them she would come and walked from her house to the meeting cursing all the way, saying if God didn't heal her, she really didn't care if she died. When she got to the corner where we were holding the meeting, she leaned on her cane as I shared the Word of God with the crowd. I was talking about the woman with the issue of blood, mentioned in Matthew's gospel. This woman had problems with her health for twelve years, the Bible tells us. She went to doctors, spent all her money, but nothing helped her until the day she saw Jesus. She believed if she could just touch the hem of His garment, she would be healed.

Disruption? Or Deliverance?

I was also preaching about Bartimaeus, the blind man. He heard the stories of the people Jesus healed and raised from the dead. When he was told that Jesus was passing by, he started to shout to Him. Jesus came to him and asked what he wanted. Bartimaeus replied that he wanted to be healed—and Jesus healed him. I also shared about my lungs, which had been destroyed by drugs and cigarette smoking. Dr. Jerry Ginsberg, who had his office on the corner of Front and Norris streets in North Philadelphia, told me I wasn't going to live another two years if I kept taking drugs and smoking cigarettes. But in 1979, when I went to that crusade and Jesus came into my life, I noticed that my mouth became very dry, and when I spit, it was clear instead of black and green like it had been.

I praise the Lord that the night Jesus saved me, He also healed me. As I shared these stories from the Bible and my own personal testimony of healing, I kept watching that woman because she was jumping up and down swinging her cane. I thought she was trying to interrupt the service. I then noticed my good friend Win Lederer and his wife, Lila, back there with her, shouting. I thought at first that they were just trying to calm her down. Then I saw a few other people from Pastor John Yamin's church approach them only to start shouting themselves! From where I stood, it looked as if they were trying to calm her down.

Instead, she was dancing, and they were shouting praise to the Lord. She kept swinging her cane, and I thought she was trying to hit the people around her. When I saw all that commotion, I stopped the message and asked Pastor Parks what was going on. His sisters and others were running toward this woman.

"Why is she interrupting the service?"

Pastor Parks then explained to me that they were shouting and dancing and praising the Lord because God had just worked a miracle in her life.

"A miracle? What do you mean?"

"Her leg," he told me, "had been black and green from the gangrenous infection. She's shouting because while you were preaching, the words came out of your mouth and went into her—that's the way she describes it. She said it felt as if fire went into her body, burning her with a 'good' sensation, and when the fire touched her leg, she was healed. Now her leg looks as normal as if she had never had gangrene!"

He'll Do it for You!

Finally, the woman was brought to me, crying and sobbing, and her wig had fallen off—but she didn't care. She was just shouting and praising God. She stamped her feet and jumped into the air. There must have been about five hundred people in that meeting, and only about sixty of us were believers—the rest didn't know Jesus Christ as their Lord. When the word spread about this woman's healing, people began streaming out of their houses to find out what it was all about. She began to tell people that God had healed her. Many people who knew her looked at her leg and realized a miracle really had taken place in her life.

When I saw this, I gave an altar call, saying, "The way God has healed this woman today—and we have the evidence in front of us—He can do the same for you!" Many people came forward for salvation—we probably had at least one hundred people at the altar for salvation alone. After that, I started praying for healing and deliverance, and even more people came to the altar. As I touched those people, I could feel the anointing of God burning in my hands. It felt as if they were on fire, and as I laid hands on the people, they would break out crying. When we saw all that was happening, we rejoiced in the Lord. Because we were so blessed by what He had done, we gave Him the praise and the glory for everything.

We finished the meeting about nine that night, but we just stood out in the street until ten or ten thirty rejoicing in the Lord. I grabbed my baby daughter, Chrissy, hugged and kissed her and showed her off to the people—I was so proud of her. All the time I had been preaching, my daughter had been right there on the altar in her carrier, and she never made a sound. She just lay there, listening to me—and she was always quiet. We took her with us to the street meetings with no fear, knowing that God was protecting all of us.

Retaliation

That night, however, I learned something vital to my Christian life. I learned that the enemy will not allow you to come into his territory and do whatever you want without trying to retaliate. He is always going to give us a fight, if not right then and there, then later on—but it will come. He will try his best to discourage us from doing the will of God in our lives. He will try everything he can to hinder us from doing what God has called us to do. I already knew one of the areas in which we were being hit was our finances. Many of the churches for whom we held street meetings were small churches. They tried their best to help by giving us an offering, but it often didn't cover all of our expenses. This never stopped me from teaming up with them to preach the Word of God. All I wanted to do was preach the Gospel and let everyone know that there is hope in Jesus Christ for them—just as I had found my hope in Him.

Later that night we went home to our apartment, rejoicing in the Lord. Damaris was busy putting Chrissy in her crib. She looked like she was almost asleep when suddenly she began to scream, and scream, and scream. She began to cry so loudly that it irritated my ears. I started to feel the powers of darkness attacking my mind. We could feel an unwanted presence had come into our apartment. And we knew it was not going to go down easily. I grabbed Chrissy out of her crib and walked through the apartment with her, singing as I did every night, hoping she would go to sleep. Now I was going to learn how the enemy wanted to try to hit my daughter.

"It's OK, Chrissy, you're okay!"

I began to pray over her. I kept this up for fifteen minutes, but she continued to scream.

"Lord! What's wrong with my daughter? Why is she screaming this way?"

Damaris asked me to give Chrissy to her to see if the baby would go to sleep with her. She told me to try to get some rest because in the morning, I had a great deal to do in preparation for the meeting the next night. My wife took our daughter into the living room and I stayed in the bedroom. Chrissy kept crying and crying as if something horrible was bothering her. I became frustrated and angry as I sat on my bed, wondering what was making her act this way. This was not her nature—she was always such a calm and quiet baby.

The Angel on the Headboard

The devil started putting thoughts in my mind, asking me, "Where is your God now? Why isn't God helping you? Look at your daughter! All of the good things done today, all the people who were saved— and look what is happening to you now!"

He kept up his mental attack. I started rebuking those thoughts in the name of Jesus as I walked around the bedroom praying. Then I sat back down on the bed, leaning my back against the headboard.

"God, I am willing to do whatever You ask of me. I'm willing to preach this Gospel. I'm willing to let everyone know about Your power. I'm willing to go into places that are dangerous, but You have to be with me! You have to help me! Look at my daughter! Why are You allowing the enemy to have his way with her?"

As soon as I said that, peace came into my spirit. It spread throughout the bedroom. As I sat there, I looked toward my daughter's crib which was also in our bedroom, and *I saw an angel sitting on the headboard*. At first I thought I was just seeing smoke in the air, but when I focused my eyes to look again, I saw the angel very clearly! He was just sitting there. He looked at me and said, "Tell your wife to put the child in the crib." I couldn't believe what I was seeing!

"Hurry, tell your wife to put the child in the crib."

When he repeated the message the second time, I looked at Damaris in the living room and told her to put Chrissy in the crib. She couldn't understand why I was saying that and told me she was just trying to calm her down. Again I told her to put the baby in the crib. Since she didn't know what I had seen and what the angel had said to me, she insisted on trying to calm Chrissy down.

I walked over to her and said, "Give her to me now!" She handed me the baby, and I put her in her crib. The moment I lay her down, she fell asleep. Damaris asked me what was going on.

"You're not going to believe what just happened! Just as I was lying on the bed, I looked at the crib and saw an angel sitting on her headboard. He told me to put Chrissy in the crib. He had to tell me twice because I couldn't believe what I was seeing at first. When he told me a second time to put her in the crib, I told you to give her to me.

When Damaris heard this and walked into the bedroom, she felt the presence of God. It felt as if God's glory had come into our apartment. We slept in such peace because I knew God was really with me. He had his angels protecting us. He had assigned angels to me and to my family. They were there in the apartment with us, protecting us.

An Angel for Chrissy

About a month after this experience with my daughter, we went to a church in Elsmere, Delaware, to preach. When I finished preaching, I ministered to some people who wanted prayer. One of the elders asked the pastor if he could pray for my daughter, and the pastor told him, "Yes." The pastor told me that the elder wanted to pray for Chrissy and asked me if that was okay with me. When he prayed for her, he began to prophesy that God had a purpose for her life, and He was going to use her and do great things with her.

"Do not fear for your daughter because God has her in a 'war tank' that has steel sides seven inches thick. No matter what the enemy sends her way, God will protect her because He has assigned an angel to watch over her."

When I heard that, I told them about what had happened to my daughter the night the woman with the gangrene was healed. I told them about the angel I saw sitting on her crib.

"Joey, the angel you saw wasn't *your* angel. That was the angel God has assigned to her."

I began to praise God because He always confirms everything He does and says to us through His Word and through His prophets. I needed to hear that prophetic word. After seeing the Lord move in such powerful ways in our street meetings, I started to ask Him questions. I knew He had angels watching over us and protecting us. But I asked Him, "Why is it that our ministry is always struggling? Why aren't there many people who have a heart to go into the streets to reach the lost? We're willing to do this, but it seems we're always struggling." Once more, God spoke to me exactly when I needed to hear from Him.

CHAPTER 10

God Takes Me to a New Level

After our experience with Chrissy and the angel, the Lord began to open many new doors of ministry. In January, 1990, my pastor at the time, Ron Breaux, told me there was a pastor's conference in Elkton, Maryland. He felt strongly in his heart that the Lord wanted me to be there. He believed the Lord had a fresh revelation and a new anointing for my life. He told me if I went to this conference, I would be blessed.

There was a problem, however. The dates for the conference were February 12-15. After he told me when it was scheduled, I explained that I couldn't go because I already had those days booked for a three-day revival in a church in Southwest Philadelphia. He looked at me seriously and said, "Listen, I feel very strongly in my heart that God wants you to go there. He has something He wants to give you. He wants to minister to your life!"

I told him I'd pray about it—perhaps I could change the dates for the revival. I always listened to Pastor Breaux because when I looked at him, I didn't see just a man. I saw God using him to speak into my life. I am convinced that the pastor's calling is to guide us and instruct us into our purpose and destiny in the Lord Jesus Christ.

When I came home that afternoon, I had some messages on my answering machine. To my surprise, the pastor from Southwest Philadelphia—where I was supposed to do the three-day revival—left me a message asking me if we could change the dates for the revival to the following week. When I heard his message, I knew deep in my spirit that God wanted me at that pastor conference. I called pastor Breaux and told him about the message on my answering machine. He gave me the details about the conference and told me I could probably stay in the dormitories the church had on the premises. I picked up a registration form from him and sent it in.

A few days later I received a confirmation that the church had a room available for my wife and me. When Damaris and I arrived at the conference, there must have been two hundred pastors in attendance—and I didn't know any of them! Pastor Breaux told me he couldn't make it to the first few services, but he would be there on Thursday of that week. Since we didn't know anyone, Damaris and I introduced ourselves and met some of the other pastors, sharing with them a little about our ministry. Even though we began to meet people, I still felt somewhat out of place.

On Thursday night, however, a pastor's wife from San Bernardino, California, ministered to us—her husband had ministered that morning. Her name was Rosella Fox, and she was the sweetest woman I had ever seen. Her hair was snow white. She looked like a true woman of God, full of His presence. When she began to preach, God used her to speak to my life. I felt the presence of God, and I could feel the refreshing of the Holy Spirit through the message she was preaching. Her message was like a story—she was a story-teller, and I am the kind of person who likes to hear stories.

The Word of the Lord Comes to Me

As she preached her message in story form, she held my attention. When she finished, she gave an altar call for any ministers who wanted prayer. She and her husband, as well as the prophetic team of ministers there, prayed for those who responded. I stood in the back. Suddenly Pastor Breaux walked over and stood next to me after giving me a hug. He told me he felt in his heart that I should go forward because God wanted to minister to my life. I was obedient, and Damaris and I went up to the altar.

Rosella Fox walked over to where we were standing and began to prophesy over my life. As she prophesied, I could hear the voice of God coming from this woman in a way that caused the tears to run down my face. She told me everything that I was going through and what God was about to do in my ministry, how He was going to enlarge it and bring people to help me. When she finished, her husband started to prophesy over us. He too prophesied everything that God was going to do in my ministry. After he had finished, Dr. B. J. Pruitt, the founder and pastor of the church where the conference was held, began to prophesy. He spoke of how the Lord was going to take me to the threshold of hell and into the den of iniquity. He said God was going to use me to bring many people out of prostitution, homosexuality, drug addiction, and spiritual bondage. He was going to use me to set them free with His power and His Word.

He Spoke What No One Else Knew

After he was finished praying for me, Dr. Eldon Wilson—a guest speaker at the conference—began to prophesy over me too. He told me my entire life. No one at that conference knew me at all. He told me I had been in prison before I came to the Lord, and I had faced death many times. He continued telling me how the Lord sent angels to come to me and deliver me because He had a plan for my life. Then he said that I would not only bring life and deliverance to people, but I would also nourish and sustain them.

When I heard these ministers of God prophesy over me, there was so much anointing upon them that all I could do was tremble before God as the tears ran down my face. When they finished prophesying over me, Rosella Fox went to my wife and began to prophesy over her, encouraging her through the prophetic word, telling her how the Lord was going to use her to strengthen me in times when I would become weary. Then Rosella's husband began to prophesy over Damaris, saying that God was going to do great things in her life.

Here are the actual prophecies given to me in February 1990 concerning my life and ministry:

The Great Days Are Ahead

Prophecy #1 by Sister Rosella Fox: *"You shall feel the needs as you have never felt them before. For out of the depths of your heart you cried unto Him and you asked Him the reason why in many areas. But the Lord is saying unto you, 'I'm going to enlarge your ministry for it shall include the children as well.' Therefore, look ye again, and the Lord shall show you that you have a harvest. Yea, the harvest of those that you have thought that God was speaking to you about. You shall look again, and you shall see their children. You shall see those of the street who need the work, and the power, and the strength, and the miracle of God in their lives. Therefore, my son, my daughter, look again for the Lord indeed shall look upon your heart's desire, and He shall begin to expand you, He shall begin to enlarge you and He shall begin to send others to help you. Therefore, be thou encouraged in your God. For you shall begin to speak the vision as never before, and as you speak the vision, others will catch it, and they will see, and they will understand, and they will stand with you. Therefore, son, therefore, daughter, the Lord says unto thee: the days ahead are great days, difficult days but great days, and the Lord shall indeed change the thoughts and concepts in your own mind and enlarge you to do the work of the Lord in the places where He shall send you."*

Clay in the Potter's Hands

Prophecy #2 by Reverend Fox: *"Lord, I didn't understand the breaking. I didn't understand the stretching. Why was it so hard? Why was it so difficult? Why was the pressure so great, Lord? Was this not the cry that came out of your heart? Was it not the circumstances you were in and the experiences you had? But the Lord would say, Victory is on the way and the hand of the Lord is stretched forth, your tongue shall be loosed and the door of utterance shall be opened, and there shall be supply for the Lord knows the cry of your heart and the sincerity of your heart and the desires of your heart.*

Has it not been these deep dealings with you, the prunings, the cutting away, even the crushing is to bring forth a vessel of honor meet for the Master's use. Remember, I am the Potter; you are the clay. I have the right to deal with you the way I want to deal with you. I have the right to test the motivation and the desire and the attitude of the heart, of the spirit. I am your God. I am your Father. I am the Potter. And as you've been the clay in my hand, there's been a molding, there's been a shaping, and it's to bring forth a vessel of honor meet for the Master's use."

The Two-Edged Sword in Your Hand

Prophecy #3 by Dr. B. J. Pruitt: *"For if you allow the burning of the Lord to rest upon you and the anointing of God to flow into your life and if your mind will be that mind of Christ, then I shall call you to thrust forth the sickle, saith the Lord God. For I see the heart's desires, and I know that you would go into the den of iniquity and you will reach into the very threshold of hell, and you will pull out those who are bound by sin and iniquity in this life, saith God. And if you will allow my Spirit to mold you and to make you, it shall make you a flame of fire and the word in your mouth shall be as sharp as a two-edged sword, and it shall pierce the darkness, saith God. And I will cause you to bring them out of drug addiction. I will cause those in the streets who have sold their bodies to turn to the Lord Jesus Christ and become proper vessels unto Me, saith the Lord. For I have chosen you, and I have put My call upon your heart and in your life, saith the Lord God. But I desire to mold you and bring you into a place where they only can see God, and my love and my mercy and my compassion as it flows through you. For my son, the day will come when you will stretch out your hand, and those who are bound in sin, those who are bound with drugs, and those who are bound with alcohol, those caught up in prostitution, at the touch of your hand I will deliver them, in a moment of time, and bring them out of their bondage into the perfect love and liberty of the Lord thy God, saith the Lord."*

Before You Knew Me

<u>Prophecy #4</u> by Reverend Wilson: *"For thou knowest well the prison in which you were incarcerated. You know the habits that had you bound and the shackles that had you sitting aside. You know the shackles that made it impossible for you to move and live a life of freedom and liberty. But did not I in your hour of darkness, in your hour of despair, even when the thoughts of suicide and the actions of suicide were in your mind, did not I come unto thee and bring deliverance? You did not know from whence it came. But yet I sent even my angels from heaven to bring deliverance unto you, and thou hast been born out of that sin, even thou hast come forth out of those shackles and out of that prison house, out of that mentality and I have done it that I may use you even as an extension of My purpose. But yet, saith God, wasn't it also true that when you were set free and delivered, there were few who cared to nurture you? Yeah, there were those who passed by, there were those who were used to bring you life and liberty but yet there was no ongoing care. But my son, I will warn thee, it shall not be so with you. For you have begun to do as you were done to, but I will stop you short in your tracks, saith the Lord God and say, you should*

not repeat that which was done to you. Yea, there were those who brought you deliverance, but they did not nurture you, they did not watch over you after, and I will warn you, do not follow in that same pattern but tie yourself unto people who can carry on the work that I will use you to bring, saith the Lord God. Do not bring life and then leave them alone, but yea, I saith unto thee, ye shall become a part of that which is able not only to bring life but should also be able to sustain and nurture it. Yea, saith the Lord thy God, you should not repeat the pattern that was given unto you, but you shall learn from the Word of the Lord, and you shall hear the counsel of the Most High God. Ye shall bring deliverance, but you shall not go alone. You shall take with you and be tied unto and work with those who shall pick up where you leave off and bring the harvest into my garden, saith the Lord."

After they had finished praying for us, we sat down again. Then everyone went to the fellowship hall to have something to eat. When we went, we were seated with a pastor we had just met at the conference, Reverend Ernest Smith. Pastor Breaux was seated with the guest speakers. Pastor Breaux began telling the guest speakers about me, and they called me over to them. He introduced me to each of them. They were all so excited that I was there and asked me to greet the people briefly the next day.

The Fresh Anointing

Friday morning, the conference leaders had a couple of pastors greet the people and tell them a little bit about their ministry and where they were from.

When I was called up, I shared what we were doing in the streets of Philadelphia and about the people who were being saved. Then I shared how the Lord called me three times by my name when I was ready to kill seventeen people and then take my own life by having a shoot-out with the Philadelphia police. I told them how the Lord used a woman in a street meeting to call me by my name, to tell me everything God was doing in my life and to let me know that God was calling me into His Kingdom.

When I finished speaking, the power of God fell in that place in such a way that people began to stand up and praise the Lord, giving God all the glory. The anointing that was coming upon my life was so strong—I could feel a fresh anointing even while I was speaking. Now I was being encouraged by the Lord Himself. That morning, after the meeting had ended, twenty or thirty pastors from Tennessee, West Virginia, Virginia, New York and different parts of Pennsylvania came over to speak to me, asking me to minister in their churches. I told them I would be glad to do that!

A New Burden From God

After the conference, I began to feel a burden in my heart to start a church. I remembered the word Dr. Wilson gave to me that God would not only use me to bring deliverance and light to those in darkness, but He would use me to sustain and nourish the people. Even though the burden was in my heart to start a church, I resisted it for a long time. I didn't want to be a pastor. On three different occasions, through three different preachers, I was told that God was giving me a pastor's heart. But I didn't want to receive it! I told those preachers they had missed God, and being a pastor wasn't my calling. My calling, I told them, was to be an evangelist, holding street meetings and preaching from church to church. They continued to tell me, however, that God was calling me into the pastoral ministry. Later that same year, in October, I was invited to speak at a revival in Rocky Mount, Virginia, where there were many pastors. Apostle Joseph Crandall came up to me and told me God was giving me a pastor's heart—one more voice from God telling me something I didn't want to hear.

During that three-day revival in Rocky Mount, Virginia, God's power moved in a mighty way as I was preaching. The Lord used me to speak to the young people who attended the Bible college they had in their church. I shared some of my testimony and my experiences with angels. When the revival was over, Pastor Kent Gerry from Ocean View, Virginia, asked me to hold street meetings in his area. I told him to get a few pastors together in January of the following year so I could meet with them regarding these meetings. He gathered the pastors together, and I met with them, sharing the burden in our hearts to reach the people in that area. Four of those pastors caught the vision to hold street meetings in their cities, and I could already see that my ministry was taking another turn.

In those meetings I met Pastor Felton Hawkins, Pastor Courtney McBath, Pastor Scott Dickson, and of course, Pastor Kent Gerry whom I'd met at the revival. We chose four days in May to conduct these outreaches. I told the pastors I wanted to hold a three-day seminar in March before the meetings to prepare the people who were going to work with me in the street meetings. I wanted to train them in the way the Lord had shown me to hold street meetings. I knew they were already trained in their own way, but there were certain things I wanted all of us to understand so there would be no strife among the workers. Workers would often try to witness and lead people to salvation while I was giving the altar call. This created confusion in those who were listening.

I wanted the people who felt led to be involved to fast and pray from March to May. We had close to three hundred people who came to the seminar where we prayed for them, anointing them to do the work. There must have been twenty different churches involved. The Philadelphia branch of the 700 Club—run at that time by Sister Mickey Nagler and Brother Win Lederer—told people in Virginia what we were doing there, and they backed us up in those meetings. As the 700 Club became involved, they hosted a luncheon to get more pastors to be part of the outreaches. About one hundred pastors showed up—many of them weren't going to be in town that week, but they gave their financial support and sent people from their churches to work with us. We began to see everything come together!

God Gives Me a Father in the Faith

While I was speaking at the luncheon, there was a man sitting at the front table who kept staring at me. When I finished speaking that afternoon, he came up to me, hugged me, and kissed me on my cheek. He called me "Son," and I could see a father in him.

"The Lord told me to tell you that because you don't have a father in the faith, that I was to adopt you as my son in the Lord."

This man was Bishop Valeriano Melendez, a powerful prophet of God whom the Lord was using powerfully in the Word and in the prophetic ministry. When we finished the three-day seminar, I returned to Philadelphia. Bishop Melendez called me to tell me he was coming to Philadelphia to see me. He lived in Ahoskie, North Carolina, at the time. When he arrived in Philadelphia, we went out to lunch with my pastor, Ron Breaux. We had a great time together, and Bishop Melendez stayed in my house, telling me many things that God was about to do in my ministry.

He told me God was going to open many doors and would give us wealth to do the work He had called us to do. After he said this, he prayed over my wife and me.

"Get ready! The Lord is placing a greater anointing upon you and your wife. You will do the work He has called you to do without being in want."

Then Bishop Melendez invited us to come to Ahoskie, North Carolina, to hold a three-day street meeting in his area sometime in June. After he returned home, the burden in my life to start a church became stronger. However, I kept fighting it because I had a hard time believing I could stay in one place and teach people; my heart was to be on the road doing the will of God. I asked Pastor Breaux if I could meet with him—I needed to tell him the struggle I was going through. I knew God was calling me to pastor a church—and I didn't want to do it.

CHAPTER 11

Yielding to God's Will

As I shared with my pastor the burden I had in my heart to start a church, he told me he didn't doubt that one day I *would* start one—but now was not the time. I accepted his counsel. A few months later; however, I called Pastor Breaux again and told him I needed to talk to him. He told me he was glad I had called him because he wanted to speak with me too.

A few days later we met at the McDonald's on 22nd and Lehigh Streets. I had Chrissy with me—she must have been about two and a half years old at the time. Before I told Pastor Breaux what was in my heart, he told me that I didn't have to say anything because he already knew what was going on with me. He told me I felt an even greater burden to start a church, and the Lord was telling him now was the time.

"The other day, the Lord would not leave me alone. He continued to tell me to anoint you and your wife. He told me to ordain you so that you could continue to do the work He has put in your heart."

Anointed and Ordained

A few weeks later Pastor Breaux called to tell me that he was moving back to Lafayette, Louisiana, where he was from originally. There was such sadness in my heart when I heard that because I knew I was going to miss him. However, he also called to tell me that he wanted to fulfill what the Lord told him to do—to anoint and ordain Damaris and me to start a church. During a service in May 1991, we were anointed and ordained.

We held crusades in Norfolk, Virginia, holding our first meeting with Pastor Courtney McBath. When I saw the table they had set up for the counseling, I asked what it was for. Pastor McBath explained that the table was to take the names of the people who would become saved. I asked him what was in the box on the table. He told me it contained Bibles to give to the new believers.

"How many are in that box?"

He told me there were thirty-two Bibles inside.

"Listen, you need to get five more tables and a lot more Bibles!"

The Harvest is Ripe

He didn't question me but had some of the people from his church bring in more tables and Bibles. The worship team ministered in music, and then it was time for me to speak. I preached for about twenty minutes, and when I gave the altar call, about two hundred twenty people came to the altar. Pastor McBath was shocked! And this was only the beginning—the second night, one hundred fifty-six people were saved. Many of these were people caught up in prostitution in the Ocean View area. On the third night of the crusade, one hundred fifty-eight people came forward for salvation, and on the fourth night, a total of one hundred ninety-one came to the altar to receive the Lord in the Newport News area where Pastor Felton Hawkins was from. The Lord was moving in a powerful way!

Many pastors became acquainted with us because of that crusade and began to invite us to come preach in their cities. The 700 Club told us they wanted to provide backing for us wherever we went to hold our street meetings anywhere in the United States. When we prepared to go to North Carolina, Tennessee, Texas, and other states, I went ahead a month early to meet with the pastors to get them ready for the meetings. After meeting with the pastors, I would then hold a three-day seminar to prepare the people in the churches for the meetings. Then from the last day of the seminar to the date of the first meeting, they would commit themselves to pray and fast for the meetings. They would be fasting for souls to be saved, for the enemy to be bound, and for us to take these communities for the glory of God.

In San Antonio, Texas, we held tremendous street meetings. The devil was furious because every night about one hundred thirty people were being saved! On the third night, two hours before we arrived at the place where we were going to hold the meeting, there was a drive-by shooting. Two young men were murdered, and three others were wounded. The police let us come into that area after all of this, and we set up the equipment we had brought from Pennsylvania and preached. About one hundred ten people were saved that night.

Changed Hearts, Changed Lives

From there we continued to hold more street meetings in Tennessee, Pennsylvania, and in New York. We even set up a missionary trip where twenty-three people teamed up with us to go to Puerto Rico and the Dominican Republic. The 700 Club funded the food and all the groceries that were to be given away to those in need. We went to areas in Puerto Rico where we were opposed by the local drug dealers who didn't want us there. I know that because of prayer and fasting, chains were broken, and when we got there, even the drug dealers came to us with cases of soda and food to give away to the people in the community. When we gave the altar call, some of those same drug dealers came to the Lord!

We held meetings in four different areas in Puerto Rico, and a total of around nine hundred people were saved in those meetings. After the meetings in Puerto Rico were concluded, twelve of the group returned to the United States, and eleven of us went on to the Dominican Republic where we also distributed food and clothing. When we gave the altar call, many people gave their lives to the Lord. One night as we were conducting a street meeting, it began to rain hard. To my amazement, no one went home. People just opened their umbrellas and stayed there to hear the message. I was soaked, and my shoes were full of water! When I gave the altar call there in Puerto Plata, Dominican Republic, people knelt down on the ground that was soaked with water until it was just mud, but they didn't care. As they knelt before the Lord, I prayed for them. It was apparent to me the Lord was taking our ministry to another dimension.

When we returned to Philadelphia, we started the church right in our office! It was big enough to start the work. We began training people for more meetings in Philadelphia. I told the Lord we needed a bigger building for the church. We used our living room which only held twenty people. We used the offices on the other side as a Sunday school. We rented this space from a pastor whose wife was a doctor. She had her offices on the first floor, and we used the second floor. God continued to send people to us, and we kept on holding street meetings. People were being saved and coming to our church.

Right on the Threshold of Hell

One day Jerry Cardona, a friend of mine, came to me and told me about a building he knew about and asked if I was interested in it. This building had been used as a night club. I asked where it was, and he said it was on 6th Street in North Philadelphia. I assumed it was going to be a building which was already fixed up and ready to be used. Instead, when I went to look at it, I saw to my horror that it was boarded up. It was in the threshold of hell, in one of the worst communities in North Philadelphia, infested with drugs. There were murders and other serious crimes committed there frequently.

I looked over the building and saw that it was somewhat bigger than what we had at the time, but it was going to take a great deal of money to make it operational. I figured it would take about $30,000 to accomplish the work. Even though there was so much to be done, the Lord gave me great peace. When I went to look at the building, I had to climb over three stolen cars and enter through a broken window. Once I was inside with my friends, Win Lederer and Will Foster, they told me it would take a miracle to get this building back in good condition. But when I looked at the building, I didn't see the terrible shape it was in; I saw the finished product.

Not $30,000 but $300,000!

Unfortunately, the kitchen ceiling was lying on the floor, and some of the first floor had fallen through into the basement. The building had no windows, it was filled with graffiti, and it had bullet holes in the walls—it looked as if it had been used as a shooting gallery. There was drug paraphernalia on the floor.

"Lord! If this is where you want us to be, then you need to provide the money to repair it!"

I brought a friend of mine, Arasu Rajaratnam—who owned apartment complexes and supported our ministry—to see the building, and he told me it would take *$300,000* to renovate the building. I was sure he had missed God or something, but he was exactly right. In the midst of everything, the Lord was at work. The Bible says the prayers of the saints go before the throne of God every day. The angels bring these prayers to the Lord.

We started to pray, asking God for His guidance. The prophetic word that Bishop Melendez had spoken over my life started to become a reality. As people heard what we were doing, they began to contribute toward the finances. A heating company donated an entire heating system. An electrician, who was also a member of our ministry's board of directors, donated the labor and material for all the electrical work we needed and even put up the panel boxes. I went to these people and asked them just what they were doing because I didn't have any money to pay for their work. They would tell me to just be quiet and move out of their way, that the Lord told them to do what they were doing. So I moved out of their way!

I started to hold fundraisers and began sending out letters to tell the people what we were doing. People began to contribute large amounts of money. In a year and a half, the building was completely renovated, debt free. We spent close to $300,000. On June 6, 1993, we dedicated the building, and Bishop Melendez was our guest speaker. Many of the people who contributed toward the renovation or did much of the work came out to the dedication. As Bishop Melendez spoke, he started to prophesy.

"My son, the Lord told me to tell you that you need not to worry because He is going to bring people. What you see here is nothing compared to what you are about to receive. For He is going to give you people to help you, and He is going to bring millionaires, and He will give you many more estates, and He is going to give you the people to help you fix them."

The Vision Surely Comes!

After the dedication, Bishop Melendez returned to his home in North Carolina and we didn't see him for another year and a half. At that time, he came back to Philadelphia, and when he got out of his car and stepped foot on our property, he said, "The prophecy has been fulfilled." One of our deacons, Keith Brockenbrough, who was also director of the men's center, asked, "Why do you say that?" But he then commented, "I guess you're right!" Keith showed the bishop the two houses adjacent to the building which we bought and renovated to be our men's rehabilitation center, spending close to $150,000. In these two buildings we were able to house about fifteen men, and we had teachers who came to the center to teach them both the Bible and also various trades.

Then Keith told Bishop Melendez we had another building around the corner on 5th Street. We owned five buildings which were adjacent to each other with a total of nearly sixteen thousand square feet that we were renovating for various outreach needs. It was going to take a great deal of money—maybe half a million dollars—to repair them. We didn't have the money, but we did have faith in a powerful God who could touch the hearts of people, who could give the money necessary to finish the work. Every day I could see the angels moving on our behalf. We were fixing up these buildings and getting them ready for a women's rehabilitation center for both single girls and for mothers with children. One house was going to be used as a missionary home, three of the houses would be turned into the women's center, and the remaining building was to be used to house our staff. From January to May things were moving right along, with the finances coming in and the renovation getting done.

However, when the summer months arrived, our finances for renovation dried up. When this happened, we would stop the renovations and go out to conduct more street meetings in different areas of Philadelphia and New Jersey. We took those summer months to witness in our communities and work with other churches. Then in the fall, I noticed our finances started flowing back in again for the renovation of the buildings. In November we stopped all work on the buildings to get ready for our Thanksgiving dinners. At these dinners we would feed close to four thousand people in two different areas. We would give them clothing and distribute at least three hundred bags of groceries to families in need. At Christmas would give toys to at least one thousand five hundred children.

The Lord was working with us to bring in a great harvest of souls. We had many volunteers from different churches who would come out and give of their time and money to help us with these activities. We held a seminar where we trained our volunteer workers for these outreaches. We had other people who raised finances and brought in clothing, turkeys, toys, and more. God blessed us with many volunteers who had His compassion for the lost souls in our area.

Bringing the Work to Completion

However, one day I realized that I felt burned out. We had been working on those buildings for two years. Though everything had been done in phases, and we already had a section open to take in girls, I knew I had to finish them completely. I didn't want to go into another year of raising funds for those buildings. We had people in our ministry working with us, and the Lord was meeting our needs. I still needed about $250,000 to finish those buildings. I went on a five-day fast, and on my fourth day of fasting, the Lord told me some things to do and gave me the names of some people to call. I wrote all of this down.

One of my friends, Jack Kreischer, had become a member of our ministry's board of directors, and whenever either of us was discouraged, we would encourage each other by sharing what the Lord was doing in our lives. Every time I saw him he was excited and enthusiastic about the Lord. His name was one of the ones the Lord gave me on the fourth day of my fast to call. The Lord said to tell him He wanted him to help me finish the renovations of the buildings. Before I called Jack, I called the three other people whose names the Lord had given me and told them what the Lord had instructed me to say. All three of them were obedient to the call of God and began assembling their teams, sending people in from their churches to donate labor. I also needed someone who could take care of the heating and air conditioning. I prayed for one of my brothers in the Lord, Charlie Keller, to see if the Lord would have him do it. As I called him on the phone, I was aware that he had a full-time job, and I didn't know how he could fit our work into his schedule. When he told me he was working full time, I told him God would work everything out so he could do the job on our building.

Two weeks later, Charlie was laid off from his job, and he called to tell me that God really wanted him to work on our building! I wanted to make sure that he was paid for the job he was doing for us as he worked the next six months making sure everything was in order.

I called Brother Jack Kreischer and told him what the Lord had laid on my heart.

"Jack, God told me to finish the renovations on this building on 5th Street. He told me to tell you to help me—I don't know exactly what He means by this.

I need to focus on what I've been called to do—and that is to continue to go out into the streets to preach the Gospel without feeling the stress of the building renovations."

"You know, Joey," Jack replied, "when you said that to me, I felt the presence of God like electricity came into my body."

God's Provision Flows In

I told Jack God said He was going to pour an anointing on him to raise the balance of what we needed to finish the renovations--$250,000. Jack began talking to people, and the anointing God told me was going to be poured into his life to raise the money became evident. Many people to whom he spoke started to send money toward the renovations because God touched their hearts to help us. A brother, who owns a construction company, began sending truckloads of materials to us. Every time we needed materials, we wrote him out a list, and he took care of it for us. He even contributed financially toward the building, going the extra mile by sending laborers two or three days to replace all the windows and doors in the building.

People asked me constantly, "Where are you getting the money to do this work? Where are you getting your grants?" All I could say was no city or state government was funding this work. The Lord God Almighty was the One who was making these things possible!

CHAPTER 12

The Angels of God Thwart the Plans of the Enemy

In October of 1998, all the buildings were completed. We had a total of fourteen properties. Four houses had been given to the ministry, and we used them for the staff to live in. We had five houses for mothers with children and single girls, and one house set up for missionaries who came to us from other cities to help with our street meetings. The other house was for the center's staff. We started a youth ministry averaging about one hundred young people. We had arcade machines, pool tables, air hockey, and basketball courts. God was moving in a powerful way. In 1998, we dedicated the building on 5th Street, and at the ceremony everyone was amazed at how well the buildings looked. When he saw the "finished product," even Brother Ruben Tarno who had donated the buildings to us said, "You did a wonderful job here, Joey. If I had known you could make them look this good, I probably wouldn't have given them to you!" But he added, "I didn't give them to you—it was God!"

The church began to grow, and we were experiencing another phase in the ministry. But there came a time that the church grew stagnant. We were being attacked constantly by people whom the devil was using. On three occasions witches came to the church, and I could see the coldness and hatred they had toward me. I rebuked those spirits in the name of Jesus and commanded them to come out. The witches would leave and never return.

Time to Move

On another occasion three people were visiting a spiritualist who lived next to the church. They happened to stumble into the church one day and became saved. One day I went to visit the woman who lived next to the church who was performing witchcraft in her house. I told her if she didn't stop all of it, the same devil that had her bound was going to take her out because God was going to destroy the works of evil in her house. I told her we were praying for her. As I was talking with her, she became frightened and started to tremble. She almost began to cry and told me she knew she had to stop. She told me her parents were Christians and part of a ministry in Puerto Rico. She had been raised in church, had backslidden, and now she was bound up in witchcraft. I prayed for her, but sadly, she didn't repent. A few months later, she moved out of her house, and we never saw her again.

The enemy made constant attempts to oppress us. People were hesitant about coming to our church because on four different occasions, there were shoot-outs right in front of the church. On one occasion a young man was murdered in front of church. Another one was murdered right in front of the center. On the corner another one was killed. We began to pray and intercede, calling on God to tear down the strongholds of violence and murder in our community. During all this, I noticed that the church was not growing; we needed to move! I kept praying that God would open up another place for us to worship.

However, as time passed, I found myself becoming weary. The work of the ministry and the centers was a heavy burden that seemed to fall on me every day. It was difficult to raise up leaders who would be strong and stay in the position God gave them. Sometimes we brought people in from other ministries to accomplish certain tasks, but to them it was just "a job." It wasn't a ministry to them, and they didn't have a heart for the work. When they found out how demanding the work was, they would leave. We continued to pray, but I was becoming discouraged. I still remembered, however, the prophecies spoken over me at the pastor conference and the ones given to me by Bishop Melendez that God would bring forth great supplies and meet the needs of the ministry.

The Man Dressed in White

One night in the summer of 1999, Damaris was sick, and she didn't go to church with me. I took my daughter Chrissy with me to keep me company. I was teaching on the attributes of God, that God was both omnipotent and omniscient and that for Him, nothing was impossible. He knows where the devil is, where his throne is, and He knows where the enemy is going and what he is planning to do. I felt such an anointing that night!

When I finished preaching, I went to my office on the second floor of the church to change my shirt; when I preach, I sweat a lot and my clothes get wet. While I was changing, Manny Gonzalez—one of my staff who was running the center—was talking to me. As we were walking out the door into the main office, Manny said, "Wait a minute, Joey, you forgot the milk and lunch meat you told me to get for your family." Waiting for him in the main office right outside my wife's office, I felt a cold wind come in through the door—so cold that it shocked me. It caused me to have cold chills run through my body. I was trying to find out where this cold air was coming from. I looked to my left and was shocked at what I saw.

A man was standing there, dressed in white. His hair looked like a cloud and flowed backward. He wore a belt around his waist and had purple linen at the collar, sleeves, and hem of his robe. He wore sandals on his feet. He looked at me, smiled, turned around, and walked away. When Manny returned and I told him about this man, we began praising God. The people who were downstairs heard us and came upstairs—even Chrissy came up to see why we were making so much noise praising the Lord.

As soon as they walked into the main office, they felt the presence of God, and they, too, began shouting and glorifying God. I told them what had happened. We must have spent another forty-five minutes in the church praising the name of the Lord. I wanted to get home to share with Damaris what happened. When I arrived at our house, Damaris was upstairs still sick and already asleep. Chrissy was so excited that she woke her mother up.

"Mommy, Mommy—get up! You have to hear what happened to Daddy!"

Damaris woke up frightened, thinking that something terrible had happened to me. Then Chrissy said, "Let Daddy tell you. He's coming up the stairs right now!" When I walked into the bedroom where my wife was sitting on the side of the bed, whatever had been afflicting her departed right then. I began to share with her what happened in the church. As I spoke with her about what happened in the church, the same presence and anointing I had felt in church came into my room. Damaris kept telling me, "I feel the presence of God all over this place. I feel better!"

We were so excited we didn't go to sleep until late that night. I was so overwhelmed with what I had seen that it was difficult for me to fall asleep. Since I couldn't get to sleep, I told Damaris to bring Chrissy to our room and let me try to go to sleep in my daughter's room. I remained excited and awake for a long time due to what happened in church. Finally, however, I fell asleep.

No Compromise!

Around three in the morning I woke back up and couldn't go back to sleep. As I tossed and turned, I felt a spiritual battle taking place in my life. Finally I got out of bed and started to pray. After praying for a half hour, I felt a presence enter the room. Then I heard a sound as if someone was in the room with me. I grew silent and stopped praying. I felt as if someone was walking toward me—and I knew whoever was in that room had to be a visitor from God. When that presence drew closer to me, I felt a great peace and a joy running through my spirit and my body. I was kneeling on the floor as it drew closer, and someone put a hand on my left shoulder. The same person put his other hand on my right shoulder and whispered into my ear.

"The reason I revealed myself to you is to let you know that whatever you do, never, never compromise."

As soon as He said that, He left, and I began to cry. I cried so loud that Damaris and Chrissy heard me. They came to the room to ask me what happened, but upon opening the door, they began to praise God and exclaim, "Someone was in this room with you!"

I told them what happened—I hadn't been able to sleep so I got up to pray. As I knelt in prayer, a man walked into the room and told me the reason He had revealed Himself to me was that whatever I did, I was to "never, never compromise." And then He left.

That morning—a Wednesday—I was preparing myself to preach in our church that night. I was sitting in my living room, reading the Word. As I studied the Bible, I felt a presence come into my house—and I knew it wasn't God's presence. I heard a voice say to me, "Joey, do you want to see your church grow? Do you want to see your church become a large one? Then you need to compromise with the people."

When I heard this voice, I said to myself, "I know this is not God!" And then I thought, "Compromise. How do you compromise? I don't know!" I stood up from where I had been sitting, went to our front door and opened it, and began to rebuke the devil in Jesus' name.

"I bind you up! You spirits that came in here are not welcome—I haven't given you authority to come into this house, so I command you to leave now!"

I had the door open, and my wife looked down the steps from the second floor and asked me what I was doing. I told her I was rebuking the devil because a spirit had come into our home while I was studying, trying to talk me into compromising!

"So I'm telling those spirits to leave!"

When I returned to my study of the Word, the Lord took me to Galatians 3:1-3. In one of those verses, Paul talks about being bewitched and asks, "Who has bewitched you?" I looked up the word "bewitch," and it means to deceive, mislead, or lead astray. I read down to verse three which says, "You had begun in the Spirit but now are trying to accomplish your goals through human effort." The Lord gave me a revelation on the spot concerning what just happened to me. He showed me if I started in the Spirit—and look how far He had brought me!—and if I stayed in the Spirit, He would take me even further than this. He would bless me in such a way that I would never be in want or lacking anything. I stood up from my study excited because the Lord was revealing to me what was about to take place, and it was the same night I had the visitation from the Lord.

The Enemy's Assignment

After that visitation I received an invitation from a friend of mine, Pastor Hector Martinez, whose daughter was getting married in Puerto Rico. I had not seen his daughter since she was a toddler. Through the years I told her I would come to her wedding. She always reminded me of that and kept me to my word. Her wedding day was Sunday, July 18, 1999. We arrived in Puerto Rico the Tuesday before the wedding, and it seemed as if the devil had an assignment on my life.

Before we left for Puerto Rico, I prayed with Brother Ruben Tarno, and he had Eliezer DeMoura, a missionary, with him. After praying for about an hour,

Eliezer stood up and said, "The devil is going to try to kill one of you." I just looked at him and laughed.

"The devil has been trying to do that for the longest time!"

This time he said the devil was going to try even harder than before because he had sent out an assignment on one of us.

A few days after that, I slipped and fell in my garage. I cut my arm right over the main vein—the doctors were shocked at what happened because if it had been cut just a little deeper, I would have bled to death quickly.

After that accident, Damaris, Chrissy, our deacon's daughter Genessa Santiago, and I went to Puerto Rico for the wedding. When we arrived on the island, I rented a car, and we drove to Dorado, a villa that Pastor Hector Martinez owned. He told us we could stay there. Everything was fine until we reached a part of the highway which drops from nearly four thousand feet to sea level. As we drove down this steep hill, the brakes on the car failed. Only by using the emergency brake was I able to pull the car over to safety. I continued to drive the car using just the emergency brake all the way to the villa. When I arrived there, I called the rental company where we picked up the car and told them what happened. They drove out to where we were, bringing us another car.

Wednesday through Friday, I was holding a three-day crusade in Caguas, Puerto Rico. The first two nights we arrived early and went over to a little store just a few feet from where we were setting up. The third night, however, we were delayed and arrived late. I was somewhat frustrated because I like to get to my meetings at least a half hour to forty-five minutes early. That day, however, we hit so many traffic jams and were slowed down by some accidents on the road. When we finally arrived, I noticed the little store was closed. I asked Pastor Angel Robles, who was coordinating the crusade, why the store wasn't open. He told me if I had arrived at 6 PM, I would have walked in on a hold-up. Three men entered the store to rob it and took money and jewelry from the people who were there at the time. Now I understood why we had been delayed.

No Weapon Shall Harm You

Sunday morning we were on our way to the wedding at about nine in the morning. We had to drive by the airport on Balderioty Avenue. On the left hand side of the road, about five miles from the airport, were the Llorens Torres projects, which were infested with drugs and violence. Not too many cars were on the road as we were driving. When we got closer to the project, I heard three pops. I thought someone inside the projects must be shooting just as Damaris yelled, "Joey, look at that man! He is shooting into the car!"

I looked to my left and saw a man who looked as if he was demonically possessed. He held a .45 Glock, and shell casings were flying everywhere as he aimed directly at us, shooting straight into our vehicle. He must have shot at least fifteen rounds at us.

I hit the gas, and we must have been doing 100 mph. I noticed other people who were driving down the street doing the same thing we were! When we were about three miles down the road, I pulled over to the side. A few other cars pulled up alongside me, and their drivers asked if I was all right. Thank God, we were. Damaris jumped out of the car to look for bullet holes, but not one of those bullets had hit us. The other drivers were shocked because the man with the gun had been shooting directly at us.

We pulled up to a toll booth and told the attendants what happened to us. They called the police—but we kept driving to the wedding. When we arrived at the church in Trujillo Alto, I asked one of the brothers why there was so much traffic outside the church.

"Joey, if you had been here forty-five minutes ago, you would have driven right into a shoot-out. A man was just killed right in front of this church!"

I told him what happened to us on the highway, and then I related what the missionary said about the devil trying to kill one of us who had been praying that day.

God's Power is Greater!

Are angels real? Do they exist? The Bible has much to say about angels—how God sends them to war for souls, how they fight battles on behalf of God's people. When I was lost, blinded by sin and crippled spiritually, I didn't know where I was going or what I was doing. I faced death many times, and today I know that God sent His angels to protect and watch over my life because He loved me and had a purpose and plan for my life. He has the same love for you, and He has a purpose and plan for your life—and He has given His angels charge over you!

CHAPTER 13

His Angels Bring Victory in the Darkest Hour

In the fall of 2005, we once again experienced great struggles in our ministry. In January of that year, a dear friend of mine, Pastor John Chapman of the Open Door Church in Chalhowie, Virginia, called me after a three-week fast. I had been in a one-week fast seeking God's direction for holding street meetings that summer in different parts of Pennsylvania, Colorado, and Florida. Many churches in those areas were asking us to hold street meetings for them.

A Time of Transition

I wasn't at home when Pastor John called me, and he asked Damaris to have me call him because he had a word from the Lord for me. She tracked me down on my cell phone and told me what he'd said. I called Pastor John back and asked what he wanted to talk to me about. He told me the Lord had given him a word concerning our ministry and me. The Lord had shown him that I must prepare myself because my ministry was going to go through transition—a time of great change. He also told me not to worry because God was going to be with me through it all.

That April, we began to feel the pressure financially. We held our banquet to raise the $100,000 we needed for the outreaches we were planning to do in different states, traveling with our whole team. We planned to take our truck, sound equipment, van, and our people to small churches that needed help in bringing people in. We set up seminars in Florida and

Colorado to equip the people in those churches so that when we arrived during the summer, everyone would know what was expected and would be effective in reaping the harvest.

People were responding, and they started to help us by sponsoring many of my books so we could give them away to the unsaved and to those who had just received the Lord in our meetings. By the end of the summer, we had held successful meetings in Colorado, New Jersey, Florida, different parts of Pennsylvania, and Philadelphia. We brought a musical group from Puerto Rico to work with us, and we rejoiced because there must have been around seventeen hundred people saved in these meetings.

But when September arrived and we began to prepare for the cold weather, we started to have financial struggles again. For some reason, some of the churches which had supported us stopped sending their support. At the time I didn't understand why they made these decisions, but later I found that someone had gone to them speaking negatively about us. Instead of coming to us to ask about these allegations, those churches just withdrew their support. Some even sent us letters saying the Lord told them to stop supporting us.

I take everything to the Lord, and when I received these letters, I went before Him and said, "Lord, you are the one who touches peoples' hearts. You are the one who gives and takes away, and if this is what You are doing, then of course, You know what is best." However, the word that Pastor John Chapman spoke came to my heart: "transition will take place in your ministry." We were not able to keep the ministry afloat. We decided to close down our men's and women's center until we could find someone to run them because we could no longer afford to pay anyone.

From Bad to Worse

We experienced worse struggles. Running our programs and operating our ministry cost around $35,000 a month. Since we had lost some of our support, we couldn't even pay our staff, and we had to let them go. It had been about a year since Damaris and I received a salary. We only received a housing allowance, and that wasn't even enough to make ends meet for our personal expenses. In spite of this, we continued to believe in God, trusting Him and knowing that He had everything under control.

I told Fred Newfield, one of the elders in my church, that we were going to form a cell group up in his area. We started it on the patio in back of his house with ten people attending a Bible study. Despite our struggles and the financial pressures I felt, I still had the peace of God on me in such a way that was beyond understanding. All kinds of creditors were calling me. The finances weren't coming in, but I continued to talk as if God had already taken care of everything. I kept believing Him, trusting Him, and teaching His Word. At my own church or at other churches that invited me to preach, I continued to encourage the people, telling them that God was able, that He would meet their needs, even when I was going through a great storm myself.

An Angel in the Window

Finally, however, one day in September, 2005, I felt the heavy burden of it all and the physical stress that came with it. When I went to conduct the Bible study at Fred Newfield's, I arrived early to have dinner with them. Damaris had gone to our church to minister that night. After dinner, as we were waiting for people to arrive, we sat under a tent on their patio. Fred's wife, Joanne, cleaned up as Fred and I sat talking, waiting for people to arrive. While I was speaking with Fred, I looked up to the second floor of his house. I saw someone standing in front of his bedroom window that faced the patio.

As I looked up, Fred looked first at me and then up to where I was staring and asked, "Is everything all right?" I told him, no, that I thought I saw something. We continued to talk. About ten minutes later, I looked up again.

"Fred, what is your father-in-law doing upstairs in your room? He's ninety years old—how did he get up there?"

As I continued to look up, I realized that this wasn't Joanne's father. Observing him more carefully, I saw that this man wore a white robe as he stood there, looking down at us, smiling. When I told Fred this, he began to sense God's presence and asked, "Who's upstairs? What do you mean?"

When he looked up, the man had disappeared. I told him a man had just been in his room looking down at us.

"Fred, I thought he was your father-in-law, but when I looked closer, I noticed that it was a man in a white robe."

Fred walked into his house as his father-in-law walked around the house, from the front to the back by the pool—we knew he wasn't the man in the window! I told Fred whoever it was, He was from God.

"God has visited your house today!"

When I said that, Joanne came into the room, asking what was going on. When we told her what happened, we began to feel the presence of God like a cloud coming into the tent on the patio. We began to rejoice. That presence settled like a cloud on us for about forty-five minutes to an hour.

As the others joined the meeting, every one of them who entered under the tent said that they could feel the presence and peace of God. We told them the experience we just had, and we started the Bible study. I was teaching about Jesus after the resurrection when He appeared to the disciples as they were walking on the road to Emmaus. When He appeared to them, He began asking them what they were talking about. They were speaking about Him and His wonders and how even some of the women from the fellowship of believers said they saw the angels standing on His tomb. One angel was at the bottom where His feet lay, and one was standing at the top where His head had been lying. They did not see Jesus, but they saw His burial clothes folded up.

As they told Jesus what they had been discussing, they were unable to recognize Him. When they arrived at Emmaus, they invited Him to come in the house and fellowship with them and share dinner. While He was eating, the Bible says when He broke bread and took the cup and gave thanks to God the Father, they suddenly understood Jesus was with them. Then He disappeared from among them.

This was the message I had already prepared to teach that evening, and when I began to speak, I was filled with excitement because of what just happened. Fred told me he had been praying, asking God to help him build an addition, a pastoral suite, onto his house so he could have a place for leaders and pastors to come rest. During this supernatural experience, I felt God was giving him peace about the addition. Fred also felt it was a confirmation from God, and when it was finished, it was a beautiful place.

The Pressure Is On

Yet our struggles in the ministry continued. In October our financial situation became even worse. I went to different churches to speak and raise support just to keep our ministry afloat. I cried out to God because the pressure on me was so strong. Every time I prayed, I would think about the pressure I was under and all the things I felt called to do that I couldn't do because we didn't have the money. I was constantly trying to find a way to condense things in our ministry, to figure out what we could shut down to cut costs and make ends meet.

At the end of the month, I tried to pray one morning about four in the morning. It seemed every time I tried to pray, it became even more difficult to do so. I tried and tried to pray. I rebuked spirits and came against the powers of darkness that were afflicting me as I brought every thought into subjection to the Word of God. The Bible says the weapons of our warfare are not carnal. They are mighty through God for the pulling down of strongholds and for bringing every imagination into obedience to the Word of the living

God. I continued to fight these spirits, trying to understand why we were going through this. I began to cry, asking God what I was doing wrong, why we were facing these things, why all of this was happening.

"Lord, I know you said we were going to enter a time of transition, but I want to know what it is You want me to do! I am willing to do whatever You want. I don't want to do anything in my human nature or by my own emotions. I want to do everything according to your Spirit!"

I began to cry so much my body trembled. I was crying from the depths of my spirit. Suddenly, I heard my bedroom door open. When I looked around to see who it was, my four-year-old daughter Ivellise was standing at the door. Sometimes when I would pray, my little daughter would hear me and wake up. She'd come in my room and lie on the sofa and fall back asleep. This day, when she came into the room at four forty- five in the morning, I called her to me. Instead of coming, she stared at me. I noticed something seemed strange about her as if something had happened to her. Again I said, "Come here," but she went back out again. I started to pray, and then she opened the door again. This time she came over to me, and I stopped crying because I didn't want her to see me like that.

"Don't Cry Daddy - Everything Is Going to Be Okay"

She sat on the sofa where I was praying, just looking at me. I wondered why she was gazing at me like that. Then she said, "Daddy, Jesus is in my room.

He came in and sat on my bed and woke me up. He told me to tell you that He is with you and everything is going to be okay. He said not to cry any more—everything is going to be okay."

"Jesus is in your bedroom?"

"Yes, He came and sat on my bed!"

I walked her back to her room, but I didn't see anyone. I asked her where He was sitting, and she said, "Right there! He came in and woke me up and told me to tell you not to cry anymore, that everything was going to be okay."

After I left her, I went to my room and told Damaris what happened. She got up to go to our daughter's room, but Ivellise was sound asleep. I began to think about what happened. I knew my little daughter looked different, as if someone had really visited her. When I went back to prayer, I began to cry again, but it was tears of joy. I believed strongly in my heart the Lord visited my home that day.

In Revelation the Lord tells us that He walks in our midst. He knows where Satan's throne is and where he lives. When He spoke to the churches in Revelation, He said, "I am the one who holds the seven stars in my right hand, and I walk among the seven golden lamp stands." He is always present. He walks in our midst. Even when we don't understand what we are going through, He is always there to see us through it.

After my daughter had that visitation from the Lord, toward the end of November, we sold one of our properties. We were able to clear every debt our ministry had, including all the vehicles and credit cards. We give God the praise, the honor, and the glory.

His Angels Are With You!

God is real. Back when I wasn't saved, I didn't believe in Him. I didn't believe in the devil either. The devil is real, but God is more powerful than he is. God has shown me throughout my lifetime that He always had angels there to protect me. Even when I was a sinner, Christ died for me. He shed His blood and demonstrated His mercy. He sent His angels to deliver me even though I didn't know He was doing it.

Today I am aware that the angels of God are with me. I feel their presence when I travel or when I am at the altar preaching. Sometimes, I feel someone is on the altar, standing close by me. When I go into the streets and the highways and byways, compelling people to give their hearts to the Lord, I feel the angels with me. When I pray and fast for the needs we have in our ministry, asking Him for His perfect will, He lets the angels go before me and bring forth everything that is needed for me to fulfill my purpose here on earth.

Are angels real? I have given you evidence through the Scriptures and personal testimonies that they are! If you believe and trust the Lord, some day you might see the angel He has assigned to you. But whether or not you see that angel, you can know without any doubt that He has given them charge over you!

This book is dedicated in loving memory of
Deacon Jake Lee Proctor and L.D Neff.

Jake Lee Proctor

Jake Lee Proctor was born on Christmas day
I knew from the moment I saw him
That he was a gift from God,
Because he was always trying
To get people saved.

He became a spiritual father to me,
When I was just learning how to walk.
He imparted great knowledge into my life
And even showed me how to talk.

He took me to the highway and byways,
Where I compel a lot of people to come.
There I shared my life story with them
Of all the evil things that I have done.

I would see the people running to the altar
To give their hearts to the Lord,
As they fell on their knees,

I could feel God's glorious power
And also that Holy Ghost breeze.

He shared with me great things
That God was going to do, he said
I would be tested and tried,
For me not to worry for Jesus Christ
Would always be there to help me go through.

The Lord took him home
At a time when I was out of town
I can hear his voice saying to me,
"Do not be sad, my son, I'm happy
Where I'm at, wearing my heavenly crown."

By: Joey Perez

L.D. Neff

L.D. was like an angel, who stood by my side,
Who encouraged me greatly
And almost made me want to cry.

Every time he called me
It was like a message from God Most High
He would always say,
"Hey brother, stay strong in the faith
And keep running the race because God is still
With you and pouring on you a whole lot of His grace."

He was always there when I needed a true friend.
When everything seemed to be crumbling
And even coming to an end.
Every time I saw him, he had a smile on his face.
He was full of God's love
And had lots of compassion for all the human race.

He would go to the prison to preach the Word of God
To help many men believe that
Jesus Christ is real and everything
Else was nothing but a facade

One day the Lord decided
To take L.D. to be now by His side.
I can see him looking down from heaven,
From that glorious place that we know
And call it God's Paradise, Way up in the sky.

L.D., you are missed by those that you loved
And all those of the next of kin, but I know in my heart
That you are a whole lot happier; standing next to Him.

By: Joey Perez

Dear Friend,

If you would like to be free from your sins and live a happy life, give Jesus Christ the opportunity. The Bible tells us in John 8:32, "You will know the truth and the truth will set you free." In John 14:14 there is another promise from God for us: "If you ask anything in my name, I will do it."

Friend, you have to confess your sins to be born again of the Spirit. Ask Jesus Christ the Son of the Living God to come into your heart right now. He loves you and is waiting for you to cry out to Him. God Bless You!

If you are interested in a DVD, CD or books of my testimony, visit us at www.worldevangmin.com or call Worldwide Evangelistic Ministries, Inc. at (215) 331-0715. This book is also available in Spanish.

He had it all. As a drug dealer and gang leader, Joey Perez had girls, money, nice clothes, nice cars, respect. But still he wasn't happy. He saw his brother killed, his friends stabbed, and his own life nearly taken several times. It was a life he loved less as time went on. In *I Lived to Tell About It.* Joey explains how God rescued him from a life of crime and pain and brought him to a place of peace, joy and what Joey had thought was impossible, forgiveness.